BOOMERANG

"What are you following me for? Hurry up—talk or I'll shoot."

The man turned to face me more squarely, moved his lips as if he were about to speak. His mouth opened a little . . .

Too late I saw the tiny, glittering metal thing he held between his teeth. The thin stream had already jetted from it as he crushed the thing between his teeth, forced the spurt of its contents. I felt the cold little drops strike my cheek. Instantly the chill changed to a stabbing sensation of heat. Searing flame flashed over the side of my face, into my brain.

Sheets of blinding light were flickering before my sight . . . and then there was only darkness!

Also by Frederik Pohl and Jack Williamson
Published by Ballantine Books:

UNDERSEA CITY

UNDERSEA FLEET

FARTHEST STAR

WALL AROUND A STAR *

***February 1983**

UNDERSEA QUEST

Frederik Pohl
and
Jack Williamson

A Del Rey Book

BALLANTINE BOOKS • NEW YORK

VL: 8 & up
IL: 7 & up

A Del Rey Book
Published by Ballantine Books

ISBN 0-345-30701-1

Manufactured in the United States of America

First Edition: April 1971
Fourth Printing: December 1982

Cover art by David B. Mattingly

CONTENTS

1

The Crested Letter

I saw my uncle, Stewart Eden, for the first time when I was all of ten years old.

He came to our home in New London where our family had always lived. The old housekeeper, Mrs. Flaherty, who was all the "family" I had left, had prepared me for his coming. But she hadn't prepared me for the way he looked.

I was standing on the porch as my uncle came unevenly up the walk. He was a huge pale giant of a man, bronze bearded, limping a little from some old scar. His voice was strangely soft.

"You're Jim," he said, and scratched his head. That was all. I don't suppose he knew much about ten-year-olds, or whether I was likely to laugh or cry or hide behind the door when he came to visit. I think he suspected that if he patted my head or even shook my hand I might burst into tears—as though I would! I had been standing alone, except for the housekeeper, as far back as I could remember.

But my uncle couldn't take the chance, because he didn't have time for tears.

He put down his battered sharkskin bag and glanced at his watch. How characteristic that gesture was! He must have done it a thousand times that first afternoon. And each time he frowned, as though the hours were racing by too fast for him, the minutes disappearing before he could put them to work.

"Come on," he whispered in his soft voice. He took my arm and led me down the steps—not like a grownup with a child, but as one comrade helps the other.

I held back. I said uncertainly, "What about Mrs. Flaherty?" The housekeeper didn't let me go off by myself, not since the day she'd found me trapped in a home-made diving bell at the bottom of our lake and had to call the fire department to get me free.

"Sink Mrs. Flaherty," he said in that chuckling, warm voice. "You're a man now, Jim. We men have a right to go off together once in a while."

I followed him with a little doubt in my mind, but the doubt was cleared up when, from the corner of my eye, I saw Mrs. Flaherty peering at us from behind the curtain. Her lips smiled, though she was dabbing at her eyes. Poor Mrs. Flaherty! She had been too loyal to the memory of my mother ever to want to take her place in my eyes—but she couldn't help thinking of me as a son.

That was an afternoon!

My uncle took me on the big, fast monorail down to the shore. I looked longingly at the amusement park as we went past, but my uncle shook his head. "No, Jim," he said, chuckling. "Merry-go-rounds and roller coasters aren't for men. Today you have to be a man. You and I are going to see something you've never seen before. . . ."

And he was right. For that afternoon my uncle showed me—the Sea.

Something I had never seen before?

Yes. In spite of the fact that every morning from my window I saw the white flecks of breakers or the slate-gray line of squalls against the horizon. In spite of the hours and endless hours my father and I had spent in catboats.

That afternoon my uncle, Stewart Eden, showed me what the sea really was. We sat there on a jetty watching the gulls, and the low, lean submarine freighters slipping through the water far out, and the waves breaking below us. And he talked. He told me strange and wonderful things; he showed me why the sea was his life—and how it could be mine.

My uncle showed me the great sea itself—the vast solid tangle of submarine deeps and peaks and cities and unknown kelp jungles, of which the part of the ocean we landlubbers can see is only the paper-thin skin. For my uncle was a dedicated man. He had given his life to the lands beneath the sea; and that afternoon, on the rocky Connecticut beaches, I began to understand why.

The sun was low behind us. My uncle finally stopped talking—not so much because he was finished (and certainly not because I was tired of listening!) as because it simply was not possible to tell the story of the sea. It was a thing each man had to find out for himself. A thing you had to live, and could never put in words.

He looked at his watch again, in that hard-pressed, almost worried way, and sighed. He put his hand on my shoulder.

"It's a whole world, Jim," he said. "And I've got to go back to it. I wish I could spend more time with you, get to know you a little better. But I'm leaving tonight."

I stood as straight and tall as I could, trying to seem older than my years. "Uncle Stewart," I said, making my voice deep and grown-up, "take me with you!"

He didn't smile and he didn't pat me on the head. He said patiently, "No, Jim. Believe me, I would do it if the thing could be done. But it would be no kindness to you. It's a hard life in the cities under the sea, Jim. There's no place for you there—yet. You've got a half dozen years of school ahead of you before you can even begin to think of it."

His hand tightened reassuringly on my shoulder as he went on: "The time will pass though, Jim. Oh, not quickly—I won't deceive you about that. It will be slow, slow. It's hard to study and watch the teacher and read the books when the sea-cities are sparkling down there, ready, waiting for you. But some things *are* hard to do in this life, and we have to do them just the same. Your father—"

He paused for a moment and looked away from me. Then he went on quietly, "Your father was a fine man, Jim. If it hadn't been for one bad break, and one bad man, it might have been him here today instead of me." He shook his head. "It isn't right to hate anybody, Jim," he said softly, the chuckle almost gone from his voice. "But some men make hating them a temptation that you just can't resist."

"You mean Mr. Hallam Sperry?" I piped up.

"I mean Mr. Hallam Sperry. Everything your father was and everything your father did was good, Jim. He, as much as any man, made Marinia a power in the world. Giant cities under the water! And your father helped put them there. And then he died, and Hallam Sperry took over." He looked broodingly out over the water. Then he shook himself and smiled again. "Time enough for that, Jim!" he said. "But your father never shirked a job, and your father's son won't either, will he, boy? So you'll go back to school and learn your lessons and get ready to be a man. Six years. And, Jim, even after the six years, the schooling won't be over. Not quite. But then—" The deep chuckle came to life in his voice—"then the schooling will be a little different."

"Different how?" I demanded, hardly understanding what this stranger who was my uncle was saying, but oddly excited and happy.

"*Quite* different!" He was grinning at me, a grin that made me forget my disappointment. "You see, Jim, people remember your father and—well, I have a few friends myself. I won't keep you waiting. If the sea is the life for you, then this is yours." He reached into his pocket. Like a king handing a gift of emeralds to a favored noble, he gave me a marine-blue envelope with a sparkling platinum crest. "Open it up, Jim. It's yours," he said.

The paper in the envelope was stiff and crinkly in my excited hands. The crest was lettered: *United States Sub-Sea Academy*. Beneath it, typed in letters of bright sea-dye scarlet, was a short message addressed to me:

Dear Sir:

An application has been made in your behalf by Stewart Eden, Commandant, U.S.S. (Retired), your authorized guardian. It has been reviewed by the Admissions Board of this Academy.

The application has been accepted.

On the first day of September following your sixteenth birthday, you are instructed to report to the Officer of the Deck of the Admissions Section at this Academy for assignment to a Training Squadron.

Sincerely yours,

Roger Shea Larrabee
Vice-Admiral, U.S.S.
In Command

I stood staring at the wonderful, the unbelievably wonderful, letter.

After a moment, my uncle's golden voice asked, "Well, Jim? Do you want it?"

I said: "Uncle Stewart, I want it more than anything else in the world."

And then, in spite of being ten years old and a grown man for the day, I think I did cry.

The six years did pass, just as my uncle had promised.

Not quickly or easily, but with that letter locked in my trunk all the time I was at school, the years passed. I had to learn a great many things to be ready for the Academy—mathematics and English and science of a dozen varieties, and languages and history and much, much more. Six years was none too long a time for the job.

But I learned them. And I learned a few other things too.

Among them I learned just who my quiet, soft-voiced Uncle Stewart really was.

2

Cadet Eden Reports for Duty

The Bermuda sun was blindingly bright. The car from the airport let me out at the coral gates as a submarine cadet, in full sea-red dress uniform, presented arms sharply.

I stood there, my bag in my hand, wondering uncertainly if I should salute. The grinning cab driver roared off, and the cadet took the decision out of my hands.

"Advance and be recognized," he rapped out.

I tried to stand at attention. "James Eden reporting," I said. "Here are my orders."

I handed over the travel documents that had come to me in the mail the week before. The cadet scanned them briskly.

"Proceed, Cadet Eden," he ordered, martinet-like. Then, for a moment, the ramrod formality dropped from his face and he smiled. "And good luck," he added, as he returned to his post.

That was my first sight of the Sub-Sea Academy.

When I walked in that gate, Jimmy Eden disappeared. Cadet Eden, J., U.S.S., was born.

The first hours went by like seconds. It was a scramble of physical examinations and questionnaires and interviews and instructions and drawing gear and equipment and finding my quarters. In the barnlike supply shed the spidery fingers of the fitting-servo roamed over my body, clicking and twittering; and in the delivery hatch of the servo my first uniform took shape.

It was the dull sea-green fatigue uniform of the submariners. Now that my patterns were on record, I could draw the rest of my uniforms as they were needed. As the arms of the tri-dimensional pantograph sketched in the blouse, and the plastic spinnerets weaved in and out to translate it into fabric, the Stores quartermaster bellowed: "Hurry up, Mister! Put it on. The tides don't wait!"

But he could have saved his breath. As soon as the hatch opened and the uniform swung out, still sparkling with drops of the chemical rinse, I was climbing into it. As the glass hatch closed again I caught a glimpse of myself. It was hard to keep a grin off my face: Now anybody could plainly see it, I was a submariner!

But the next storesman was barking at me already; I had no time to admire my reflection.

I stumbled out of the Stores shed, grunting under almost a hundred pounds of gear, the tools and badges of my new life. As I reached the door the Caribbean sun seemed like a furnace door gaping a yard above my head. The heat, after the cool, large shed, was like a physical blow.

It was a hundred yards across the quadrangle to the dormitory to which I had been assigned. By the time I got there I was staggering.

Perhaps the sweat in my eyes was the reason I didn't see the scarlet-tuniced upperclassman who made a shipshape right turn and started up the steps just ahead of me.

I stumbled into him.

My gear fell all over the steps. I groaned, but I said, "I'm sorry," although a little grouchily, I admit. I bent down to pick up my cap.

"Atten-HUT!"

The whiplash of the word cleared my foggy brain like magic.

I leaped erect. "Sorry, sir!" I said smartly.

The cadet on the steps above me looked down with an expression of distaste. He was as tall as I, and heavier in build. His eyes under the flat scarlet dress cap were cold; somehow they seemed almost dangerous.

"Keep your mouth shut, Mr. Lubber!" he rapped. "When an officer or an upperclassman wants to know if you're sorry, he'll ask you. Don't volunteer the information. And stand at attention, Mister! Full attention—your arms at your sides."

"But I'll drop my cap," I objected.

"Mis-ter Lubber!"

"Yes, sir!" I let my arms drop. The cap slipped to the ground again. My luck had held once, but on the second fall the crystal visor shattered.

The upperclassman paid no attention.

He stared coldly at me for a moment, then descended the steps and walked slowly around me. When he had made a complete circle, he shook his head.

In a conversational tone, he said:

"I have seen a great many undesirable specimens in my life, Mr. Lubber, but I have never in two years, three days and thirteen hours at the Sub-Sea Academy seen any person, beast or thing—and I may say that I am by no means certain which of these classifications you belong in—which showed as little promise of ever becoming anything close to barely possible material for making a third-rate pump-hand's second assistant helper as you." He shook his head. "If I were to call you a disgrace to the country, to the Service and to the Academy, Mr. Lubber," he went on, "I would be guilty of gross flattery. It is on the face of it clearly impossible that you will last as long as two weeks in this Academy. I should not bother to take an interest in you at all. I am wasting the Service's good time by doing so. But, Mr. Lubber, a good submariner is charitable. My kind heart forces me to do what I can in order to protract your useless and unpleasant stay with us as much as possible. Therefore, I will take an interest in your education." He planted his hands on his hips and stared at me. "To start out with, Mr. Lubber, I invite you to learn Rule One. Would you like to learn it?

You may answer in two words, each of one syllable, the second being 'sir.' "

My jaw muscles were trembling—whether from rage or nervous laughter I couldn't tell. Obediently I said, "Yes, sir."

He nodded briskly. "Very good—that is, very good for you, considering. You answered me in more or less proper form, and it was the first time you tried it, at that. I congratulate you, Mr. Lubber. There may be some hope for you after all. It may be as long as three weeks, perhaps even three weeks and two or three days, before the Fitness Board is forced to the conclusion that you are utterly unfit to touch the sludgeboots of a real submariner and throws you out. However, let us get on with Rule One. Attention to orders, Mr. Lubber! Rule One is: 'Whenever in the presence of an upperclassman, you will stand at strict attention until he either gives you leave to do otherwise or signifies, by departing to a distance of at least five yards, that he no longer has any interest in what you do.' Do you understand that?"

I started to say, "Yes, sir," but closed my mouth again in a hurry. He had not given me leave to speak. I was learning the rules.

But I wasn't quite fast enough. He stared at my jaw in an absorbed way.

"Facial tic," he mused to himself. "This person is physically sub-normal too, it would appear—as well as mentally, morally, emotionally and otherwise." He sighed. "Well, enough of this. Mr. Lubber, it is well known that memorizing difficult rules, particularly those containing forty-five words, requires absolute concentration. To help you achieve this condition, I am permitting you to walk off fifteen tours around the quadrangle. Don't thank me; I'm glad to do it for you. It's for your own good. It has nothing to do with punishment, but is only designed to help you concentrate." He nodded with an expression of cold satisfaction. "However," he went on, "the question of punishment must also be considered. For conduct unbecoming a sub-sea cadet—to be specific, trampling an upperclassman—you may walk five additional tours. And for wanton destruction of government property—" his eyes flitted to my crushed visor—"ten tours more. You have wasted enough of my time, Mr. Lubber; kindly start on this at once. The tides don't wait!"

Without another word he about-faced and mounted the steps.

That was my introduction to the Sub-Sea Academy. I didn't even know his name.

Thirty times around the quadrangle, which is a hundred yards on a side, is seven miles.

I made it. It took me a little more than three hours, and the last few laps were in a state of near-coma.

At the twenty-fifth lap it crossed my mind that no one was counting the laps but myself. At the twenty-seventh I had to fight myself to make my legs carry me on, around that dizzying square.

But plain, homely stubbornness kept me going. The Academy was for honorable men, and—even though at least one upperclassman was obviously a sadistic brute—I was going to follow every order I received to the letter, as long as I wore the uniform.

But, at last, it was over.

I picked up my scattered gear where it lay. Dozens of cadets had climbed the steps while I was walking my tours, but none had given it a glance. I found my way to my room.

As I opened the door, a short and astonishingly young-looking lubber like myself jumped to attention. He relaxed when he got a look at me.

"Oh, you must be Eden," he said, sticking out his hand. "My name's Eskow. Tough luck; I saw you out there."

He was grinning; I liked the friendly look of his grin. "I guess you got a head start on all of us," he went on. "Well, you won't be the last. We'll all be out there sooner or later. If I know me, I'll be one of the 'sooner' ones,— and often."

I mumbled something and dumped my gear on my cot.

It made an untidy picture. The unmade bed, with clothes and books and equipment strewn all over it—as untidy and unkempt as I felt.

I looked across at Eskow's bed. It was neatly made, with an extra blanket taut across the pillow; his footlocker lay with the lid open, showing all his equipment ship-shape and stowed away. Eskow himself was pink-cheeked from a bath and shave ... though, at a guess, he could have skipped the shaving for quite a while before the fact became obvious.

I must have shown my feelings.

"Cheer up," said Eskow. "I'll give you a hand. We don't have anything to do until dinner, and there won't be any inspection till after we eat. Take a breather."

I slumped in the chair while Eskow began cheerfully to sort and stow my possessions. In a couple of minutes I began to feel better and got up to help him. It would be a long time before the soreness went out of my feet; but it looked like all my luck today was not bad. If Eskow was going to be my roommate for the next four years, judging from the first look I had at him I could call myself a lucky man.

At dinner that night I saw the upperclassman again, sitting by himself at a little table at the end of the dining hall. I nudged Eskow and pointed to him.

Eskow whispered, out of the corner of his mouth —first-year cadets were not permitted the privilege of conversation at meals—"Sperry's his name. Sorry to say it, Jim, but he's our Exec. You'll be seeing a lot of him until he graduates." Eskow hesitated. "Sperry," he repeated, looking ramrod-straight ahead of him. "I wonder if he could be——"

One of the upperclassmen was looking our way, so Eskow never did say quite what he wondered.

But I knew. And the answer was yes: Executive Cadet Officer Brand Sperry, Cadet-in-Charge of Fletcher Hall, was the son of Hallam Sperry, the millionaire mayor of Thetis in Marinia.

Something about young Sperry's face had seemed familiar to me at the time—familiar and, oddly, almost dangerous. At the time I couldn't quite place it.

But now I knew. I had seen Hallam Sperry's picture many times, and the cadet at the little table now looked like Hallam Sperry when the picture was taken—a picture of the older Sperry, my own father and my Uncle Stewart, when all there was of Marinia was a couple of tiny sub-sea outposts and all three men were young, long before the bitter struggle that divided Sperry from the Edens—

Long before my father had died, his name famous and bright, but his fortune and holdings gone.

I lifted my fork to my lips in the approved square-rigged motions of the Academy—where the combined heritage of old Annapolis and West Point and the Air Academy in Colorado produced a wealth of tradition and a thousand rules to bewilder first-year lubbers like myself. But I hardly tasted the food.

If the son of the man who had defrauded my father and tried to do the same to my uncle was going to be my commander, I had a hard mission to accomplish in the Sub-Sea Academy. And our first meeting, certainly, had been a bad start. Could it have been that he recognized me—that he deliberately picked the quarrel to make sure I knuckled under?

I couldn't believe it. No matter what Brand Sperry's father might be, the son was a cadet officer of the Sub-Sea Service, and while we were in service together there would be no trouble between us of my making. I promised that to myself, on the spot.

All the same, I did not enjoy my first evening meal in the Sub-Sea Academy.

3

Sons of the Sub-Sea Fleet

Reveille was at 4:45 in the morning. The stars were still out!

We stood there in the pre-dawn light, three hundred of us, shivering and trying to stand at attention. We must have been a strangely lubberish sight in the sacred grounds of the Sub-Sea Academy. I can hardly blame Cadet Captain Sperry for his expression of disgust.

After roll-call, we returned to our quarters and got ready for inspection. After an enormous meal—getting up before daybreak did wonderful things to your appetite!—we fell out for the beginning of our first day of training.

Every one of us had been primed for that first day from the age of ten or twelve on. We were as fit and ready as any first-year class of teen-age youths could be. Each of us had studied as much of the basic subjects we would have as our young heads could hold—and not only the mathematics and science and naval lore, but a curious assortment of widely varying studies, from art to engineering, from ballistics to the ballet. For years the tendency in schools was more and more to specialize—but for us, the future officers of the sub-sea fleet, the whole world of knowledge and learning was ours to grasp.

We were ready. And we went right to work, sweating

on the athletic fields in our fatigues, at rigid attention at our desks in our undress whites, parading across the drillfields in our high-visibility dress scarlet tunics.

It was hard work.

It was intended to be hard. No weakling could rise to command a sub-sea vessel. The service could not afford it. One moment's weakness or hesitation might mean destruction, down in the mighty depths of the sea, where the enormous weight of miles of water overhead could crush any steel or iron object like cardboard. Only one thing made it possible for our submarines to cruise twenty thousand feet and more below the surface; only one thing kept the dome cities of Marinia alive.

The name of it was: Edenite.

Bob Eskow was the first of my classmates to connect the word "Edenite" with the name of his roommate, Cadet James Eden. He asked me pointblank if I were related to Stewart Eden, the inventor.

In the years since I first saw my uncle, I had found out what the name of Stewart Eden meant. I tried to keep the pride out of my voice as I said: "He's my uncle."

"Uncle!" Bob was impressed. He thought for a moment, then ventured cautiously, "There's a story that he's working on something new, something——"

"I can't talk about it," I said briskly—and it was true, I couldn't, because I didn't know anything about it. There had been stories in the paper now and again about what Stewart Eden was up to in Marinia. But what I saw in the papers was everything I knew; what little I heard from my uncle was about me and my schooling, not about him and his work.

Eskow didn't press the point. I could see, on his open face, the exact moment when he had remembered that between the Eden family and the Sperry family there was reported to be trouble. . . .

The word got around rapidly, and before a week was out half the class was laying bets on how long it would be before there was an open outbreak between the Exec and myself. The story of Hallam Sperry's struggle with my father and uncle was public knowledge. But my uncle had taught me, in his infrequent letters, that a wise man does not hate; and I was trying to live up to his advice in my relations with Brand Sperry.

I talked it over with Bob Eskow, one afternoon when classes were over and we had half an hour to ourselves before the evening meal. We were sitting on the sandy lawn outside the mess hall, watching the giant cumulus clouds boil up over the water. Eskow said hesitantly, "Maybe you ought to talk to Sperry, Jim. It might clear the air."

I remembered by first encounter with him on the steps of the Hall. "He doesn't like lubbers," I said.

"That's the chance you have to take. That is, if you want to. It's your problem, Jim. I can't tell you what to do. But I know that it's causing a lot of talk."

I put it off. In one week I had learned one thing for sure: Lubbers did not bother upperclassmen without an invitation. In any case, I thought, the talk would die down. The struggle between Hallam Sperry and the Edens was old stuff—the break had been long before I was born. Why revive sleeping dogs?

I didn't know how wakeful that particular sleeping dog was!

But I had little time for personal problems, and as the days went by the talk did die down. We began to shape up as cadets, instead of bewildered civilians; we worked and studied and exercised and, little by little, began to show what we were made of.

I said that three hundred of us started the course. Within the first month, twenty-five had washed out. Some couldn't stand the physical strain; some couldn't seem to master even the basic scientific studies of the beginning of our first year; some could not take the discipline. Twenty-five was not a large number—it was almost certain that, by the time our class of three hundred came to graduation and the commissioning ceremony, fewer than a hundred would be left.

For the service could not afford weaklings.

Those who washed out were snapped up, by and large,

by the commercial sub-sea lines. Merely passing the entrance examinations for the Academy was proof of a strong aptitude for sub-sea command. Of the two hundred who washed out of an average class, at least half would become maritime officers in a civilian capacity.

I wondered often if I could make the grade. Just the list of our studies in the first year was frightening: Undersea mining. Submarine motor and hull design. Vau'lain cell operation and repair. Troyon tube-lights. Synthetic air generators. Submarine architecture. Eden generator maintenance and overhaul.

Of course, I had a head start. In the first class on the Eden generator, Eskow was frankly envious; after all, my uncle had invented it! But, of course, the knowledge of how to balance the circuits and check the relays and gauge the capacitances of the weirdly complex Eden generator did not run in the blood. I knew what Edenite was, of course—but so did everyone in the class.

What did help very much was the years of patient schooling my uncle had put me through before I entered the Academy. The scientific courses were much less difficult for me than for most of the class—I had taken the essentials already, in a civilian school where the pace was slow and the pressure infinitely less than at the Academy. At the top of the front wall in every classroom the motto was lettered: The Tides Don't Wait. The whole Academy was built around that principle; we had to absorb in a single semester courses that civilian universities took four years to present.

But some of the courses were completely new to me. There were classes on naval warfare and tactics; the employment of naval aviation; military and naval logistics and supply. There were ordnance classes where we had to learn and recite the range, purpose and characteristics of every weapon that could conceivably be used by or against a sub-sea warship, from torpedoes to atomic dust. There were interminable classes on the strategy of naval operations; on the infinitely variable tactical problems of sub-sea operations, far more complex than any other military operation known to man since it was conducted in three dimensions.

And there was the infuriating detail of Academy discipline to keep in mind every minute of every hour of the day. There was never a second while we were on the Academy grounds (and in that first year we could be off them a maximum of three hours a week—if we weren't confined to quarters for some infraction) when we were not liable without warning to find ourselves confronted by some officer or upperclassman hot on the trail of an unshined shoe or a failure to make a square turn going around a corner. We never walked anywhere—we marched; we never lounged back and relaxed, even in our own rooms—we sat at attention. We learned all this the hard way—in the long hours of walking punishment tours around the quadrangle, sometimes a hundred or more of us out there at once. But we learned it. And we never forgot.

For twenty-three hours and thirty minutes out of every day, this was true; but there was the half hour just before the evening meal when, if we weren't catching up on our punishment tours or frantically boning up for a quiz, we could wander about the grounds as we liked. That half hour, the three hours liberty on Saturdays and the short time between chapel and lunch on Sundays were all of our leisure time. And it was always eaten into by some extra duty.

But what was left was worth while.

The Sub-Sea Academy is a very junior institution, when you compare it with Annapolis, from which it sprang, or ancient West Point. But it has a history and a pride of service; and the grounds of the Academy are filled with trophies of the Sub-Sea Fleet.

Eskow, for instance, was obsessed with the hulk of the old SSN-571—the *Nautilus*, first of the atomic-powered undersea cruisers. He dragged me there as often as he could and we spent hours of our brief leisure wandering through its cramped corridors and chambers, where it lay moored in the gentle Caribbean swell. It was hard to believe that this fragile tin-can had once been the pride of the Navy; compared with the least of our modern sub-sea corvettes, it was pitifully small and weak. Of course, the builders of the *Nautilus* had done the best they could with mere steel for its hull and plating; they hadn't begun to guess, when *Nautilus*'s keel was laid, that my uncle would develop the thin film of Edenite that, by forcing the pressure of the water back upon itself instead of trying to hold it out by brute force, tricking the pressure itself into furnishing the necessary strength, would make it possible to plunge four miles below the surface.

My own favorite, though, was Dixon Hall. All the history of the sub-sea service was concentrated in this quiet little hall, from diagrams of the sinking of the *New Ironsides* back in that bloody October of the Civil War, the first successful submarine action of history, through the imposing Honor Roll of Academy graduates who had given up their lives in the Service. One whole wall was taken up with a map of the world, on Mercator's projection—a strange map, for the continents were a vacant black, with only the rivers traced on them in white and a few great cities indicated. But every detail of the ocean floor was recorded minutely. Various shades of color marked the depths; submarine mountains and ridges stood out in relief. I spent hours tracing the lines that showed the routes of the sub-sea traders, the thin web that showed the pipelines and vacuum tubeways that carried the wealth of the sea. All the domed cities of Marinia were there—Eden Dome and Black Camp and Thousand Fathom and Gold Ridge and Rudspatt and a hundred others. I looked longingly at the dot that marked Thetis, far into the South Pacific, where my Uncle Stewart lived and performed his mysterious duties—for he never discussed his work with me, only mine.

There was incalculable wealth there on the floor of the sea—three times as great an area as all the continents, and three times as wealthy! The shaded zones and colored patches showed tracts of minerals—oil fields, gold sands, coal beds, seams of copper and zinc and platinum. Marked in warning red were the uranium mines, the lifeblood of the world's powerlines and, particularly, of the Sub-Sea Service, for without atomic energy from the raw uranium our vessels would be as surface-bound as the ancients. It was a sobering experience to see how few and sparse those flecks were; every one of them was being worked intensively, and the supply, the rumors said, was running low.

But most exciting and provocative of all were the patches of pure, featureless white in the middle of the sea. For they are the unexplored Deeps—the Philippine Trench, Nares Deep, the Marianas—six miles, seven miles and more straight down, beyond even the range of our most powerful exploring cruisers, untouched and almost unknown. On the giant map the patches of color that marked mineral deposits seemed to grow thicker and larger as the depth increased—up to the very edges of the unexplored white. It was, they said, natural enough: the heavy minerals settled farthest down. What treasures the Deeps must conceal!

There were treasures enough, though, in Dixon Hall itself—cases of pearls and sea-amethysts and coral, the great pieces of ivory from the deepest plumbed abysses that scientists said were the tusks of ancient sea-monsters. I think that within the range of my eyes, as I stood in the center of the Hall, must have been a million dollars' worth of precious gems—with never a lock or guard! Truly, the honor system at the Academy was strong!

It was a wonderful, absorbing, exciting place. Most wonderful of all to me, though, were the ranked masses of cabinets and cases where the history of undersea navigation was on display. Beebe's tiny bathysphere was represented, and the doomed *Squalus*, and the old German *Deutschland* and many more, in carefully precise models. And there was one thing more: the tiny model of my uncle's first, crude cylindrical Edenite diver.

I think I piled up more demerits in Dixon Hall than anywhere else in the Academy—standing transfixed before some model or map, until the ship's bell announced the dinner formation, and I arrived at the lines before our quarters, breathless and racing, in time to be gigged by some officer or upperclassman for being late. It was costly

of my leisure time, walking off the demerits on the Quad;
but it was worth it.

Eskow was usually beside me as we circled the Quad.

It was hard for me to understand what forces drove
Bob Eskow through the grinding years of the Academy.
In his family was no tradition of the sub-sea service as in
mine; his father owned a newsstand in New York, his
grandparents had been immigrants from some agricultural
community in the Balkans.

The question, when I brought it up, embarrassed him.
He said, almost shame-faced, "I guess I just wanted to do
something for my country." And we let it drop. But
Eskow was always there with me, prowling through the
Nautilus or pondering the unmarked Deeps, beyond the
four-mile limit where Edenite no longer could turn the
force of the water back on itself. I didn't realize how
much I was coming to depend on Eskow's cheerful deter-
mination and quiet friendship.

I didn't realize it—until it was gone.

4

Man Missing

Within the first month we were actually going beneath the surface of the sea.

True enough, we were not going very far. But squad by squad, we drew diving gear—aqualungs, face-masks, pneumatic guns and frog-flippers—and set out on our first undersea expeditions.

I was in Crew Five, with twenty others, under Cadet Lieutenant Hachette. When we had drawn our gear we boarded a whaleboat and stood out to sea. We were not quite out of sight of land—Bermuda was a low line on the horizon—and when Lt. Hachette gave the order to stop the engines. We drifted, bobbing gently on the Caribbean swell until, at the lieutenant's command, we went over the side, one by one.

The water was shallow there—not more than twenty feet—and crystal clear. We wore regulation weighted shoes, carefully balanced to each man's weight and body volume. With them on, we exactly balanced the weight of water we displaced. It was like hanging suspended like Mohammed's Tomb. At the flick of a webbed foot we climbed; at the merest stroke of the arms, we sank.

We gathered in ranks on the rippled, sandy bottom and waited for orders.

Talking, of course, was out of the question. Standing there, teetering gently back and forth like a pillar of smoke on a still day, I was conscious of the absolute silence. The only whisper of sound that came to me was the ripple of bubbles from my breathing gear. I found out later that this was unusual—the bottom of the sea can be a very noisy place! Fish are not the mute beasts they seem; and, as I can testify, being within range of a battle royal between a hammerhead shark and a squid is about like being on the fringe of two fighting wildcats.

But that morning off Bermuda, I felt as remote as the spaces between the stars.

Lt. Hachette looked us over to make sure everything was in order; signaled us to check our gear for leaks or malfunctions; then ordered us on. In columns of twos, we marched off along the sea bottom. Curious march—in slow motion! We were at route step, and the uneven footing made it a struggle to keep in some sort of proper dress. Stumbling over sand mounds and broken branches of coral, dodging the wicked little sea anemones, that look like chrysanthemums and sting like hornets, we must have been a ludicrous sight to the curious little fishes that swam in schools overhead! It was more a ballet step than a march; half the time my right foot was off the ground before my left foot had touched before me, in a slow, stately *grand jete* that Nijinsky would have envied.

I doubted that we were making more than a mile an hour. We had air, that first dive, for only thirty minutes; we marched about a thousand yards in all, a hundred yards in one direction, then a sharp right turn and a hundred yards more. At the end of the thirty minutes we were back where we started; Lt. Hatchette gave us the signal, and we, two by two, slipped upward toward the waiting whaleboat.

It sounds rather dull, perhaps.

It was not! Every second of that first half hour was pure adventure, and unbelievable excitement. It was not dangerous excitement—we were, after all, only twenty feet down! Even though Bermuda's waters teem with sharks, they rarely go near humans, and certainly not

when the humans come in groups of twenty. But it was an
enchanted land we were traveling, inhabited by long-
legged starfish and slow sea-cucumbers and pulsing spong-
es and brilliant-colored, inch-long fish by the uncounted
thousands.

We dived twice more that day, and then the whaleboat
started back. It would be two weeks before our turn
would come again; but already I was making plans for the
next time. For I had been on the sea-bottom . . . it was
like going home again, after a long, long time away.

Cadet Captain Sperry, from the lead whaleboat, bellowed: "Attention all boats! Stand by for diving!"

The whole class was out in whaleboats; it was our first
night maneuver underwater, and it was a mass affair.
Fourteen whaleboats strung out behind Sperry's lead
boat; a score of cadets was in each boat.

It was well after sunset, though the Western sky was
still faintly glowing, and the air was getting cold. We put
our gear on in silence, then sat at ease while Captain
Sperry and his crew chiefs settled their last-minute plans.

Overhead the stars were big and clear. The Milky Way
looked like a smear of luminous paint; Orion's Belt lay
almost at the horizon and Mars winked red overhead. The
starlight seemed captured in the water itself; but it was
not reflected light that made the waves sparkle and shine,
but their own luminescence. Eskow whispered: "You think
it will be as bright as that down below?" I shook my
head. I didn't know for sure, but it seemed to me that I
had heard the luminescence was only at the surface. I
didn't know—so many things about the sea I didn't
know!

But I was learning.

Overwater the water the call came: "Attention all boats!
Check gear! By the numbers—air valves!" There was a
multiple snorting from all the boats as every one of us
valved a breath of air out of the aqualungs. "Lights!" A
couple of hundred fireflies flickered over the water as we
checked our headlamps. "Face masks!" I slipped my

mask on, along with all the others; I ran my fingers over the line where the rubber made contact with my flesh.

Everything was in order. There was a moment's pause, then Sperry's voice came: "Boat commanders, send your crews down!"

We slipped over the side.

It was absolute blackness beneath us.

As soon as the water had closed over my head, the stars were gone; bright as their light had been, it did not penetrate the surface of the sea. I could see clearly the headlamps of the fourteen crews; it looked like a convention of fireflies. But I could not see a single human figure or object, only the lights; then my eyes grew better adjusted, and I began to make out shadowy shapes moving through the water beside me under the glowing lights.

We assembled at the bottom, as usual; but there was no marching in store for us. This was a maneuver problem, designed to familiarize us with the problems of hand-to-hand sub-sea combat if we should ever need to use it. Six crews had been designated the Invaders; the other eight, Defenders. It was our job, as Invaders, to pass through the Defending line. If we were intercepted, we were "dead"; the success or failure of each team would be judged by the number of Invaders who got through without a challenge.

The Defenders were grouped a hundred yards away. At the signal, they doused their lights—and totally disappeared, as far as any of us could see. Our crew officer signaled with his light, and our crew rose from the bottom and began swimming to the attack. We swam several yards before, according to our plan, we all doused our lights simultaneously. That had been Lt. Hachette's idea— we would let the defenders see our line of travel; then, when the lights went out, we would strike out in a different direction.

Our crew was the last to turn off its lights. When they were gone, each one of us was utterly, completely alone.

Then the exercise began to seem more serious to me. It had appeared such a simple-minded child's game, when the lieutenant explained it to us, in a lecture hall, back on the surface. A sort of underwater tag—nothing for grown men to play at! But in the darkness and alone, swimming through ink toward nothingness, I began to see just how difficult it was. First, there was some element of danger; the big predatory fish, the sharks and mantas and barracudas and so on, would seldom attack a human—but in this darkness, how could they tell what we were? True, the lead whaleboat was equipped with microsonar search gear; if anything the size of a shark came within a quarter of a mile of us at any rapid rate, the underwater alarm would sound and we would abandon the exercise. But—well, just suppose the sonarman missed up?

But there were more than two hundred of us; there was safety in numbers, even if something did go wrong. What was worse than the slim chance of trouble with a shark was the blind, helpless struggle itself. It was suspended in nothingness; there was no up and no down, no way of telling if I were swimming in the proper direction or off in some crazy angle. I remembered the experiences of the daylight dives and all the long lectures I had listened to; and I tried to relax, tried to "sense" with my body and blood and the canals of my ears when I was swimming level with the bottom. It wasn't easy; I found out later that a dozen cadets had swum straight into the bottom that night, while twice as many had, to their astonishment, found themselves breaking the surface in their first halfdozen strokes.

I tried to listen for the faint whisper of someone else's aqualung bubbles; I thought I heard them, and then they were gone. I thought I heard them again, but I was completely unable to guess whether they came from ahead of me, behind, on top or below. I strained my ears to listen. . . .

And a rapid brassy gong began thundering in my ear drums. For a moment I was startled almost out of my wits; then I realized what it was.

The emergency alarm! Sharks had been sighted on the microsonar—the exercise was automatically terminated and we were to get back in the whaleboats *pronto!*

All around me lights began flickering on, flashing up-

ward like bubbles in a glass of sparkling wine. I turned on
my light and headed up too. At the surface, the silence
was gone as though it had never existed. Voices were
yelling, bellowing, growling, shouting; it was bedlam.
Over the raucous shouting came Captain Sperry's bull-like
shout: "Take your time! Get into the right whaleboat!
You've got plenty of time! Everybody get into his own
whaleboat—anybody in the wrong boat gets ten tours
around the Quad. Take your time! You'll all be in the
boats in two minutes, and that's plenty of time!"

I jerked the face-mask off my head and trod water,
staring around. I was in luck—the triple green lights that
marked Crew Five's whaleboat was only a few yards
away. A half-dozen strokes brought me to the stern; I
clambered aboard and helped the next man in after me.

The shouting and splashing began to quiet down. "At
ease!" shouted Sperry from the lead boat. "Crew commanders, report when ready!"

The voices of the commanders of the individual whaleboats began to come in. "First crew all present!" "Second
crew all present!" "Eighth crew all present!"

Lt. Hachette made a rapid headcount by the light of
his lamp. "Nineteen," he said worriedly. "Who's missing?
Sound off, men! Roll call!"

The voices came back to him. "Degaret!" "Dodd!"
"Domowski!" "Dowling!" "Dunphy!" "Duxley!" "Dyan-
osky!" "Dye!" "Ealy!" "Eckstrom!" "Eden!" That was
me; and I waited to hear Bob Eskow, next in order.

I didn't hear him. I looked around, hardly believing it,
though there could be no doubt.

Bob Eskow was not in the boat.

Already Lt. Hachette had made a swift check of the
rest of us. Then, through his megaphone, he hailed the
lead boat. "Crew Five missing one cadet! Cadet Robert
Eskow out of boat!"

There was a ripple of sound from the fourteen boats.
From the lead boat, Captain Sperry called: "Cadet Eskow!
Report!"

There was no answer.

The giant searchlights went on and scoured the surface

of the water around us, looking for a head, the stroke of an arm. ... There was nothing. Two hundred and sixty-eight cadets had set out; two hundred and sixty seven were in their boats.

Bob Eskow was still under the surface of the water.

5

Sub-Sea Search

Cadet Captain Sperry didn't even ask for volunteers.

The sharks—if it had been sharks that the microsonar spotted, and not porpoises or drifting logs—never bothered us as, by crews, we recharged our aqualungs and slipped over the side. The exercise was forgotten; we grouped in crews at the bottom, lights on, and organized a search.

It looked bad for Bob Eskow, but not—I told myself—necessarily fatal. He had air for thirty minutes; if he had merely wandered off and failed to hear the recall signal (though that was next to impossible), he would get back by himself; if somehow he were trapped, we should be able to find him in plenty of time. . . .

But if his aqualung had failed, it was probably already too late.

Over our heads, the whaleboats began dropping floating emergency flares; the flamed like little suns, bobbing a fathom or so beneath the surface, lighting up the whole sea bottom. In orderly squads we patrolled the bottom, following the hand signals of our crew leaders. The leaders blinked code signals back and forth between themselves with their headlamps, and gradually the entire class was spread out from a central point, searching the sea bottom underneath his own swimming form and for a couple of yards on either side.

Bob could hardly have got more than half a mile from the drop point, and there were almost three hundred of us. Swimming porpoiselike through the eerily lighted waters, plunging down to investigate the kelp valleys and the coral caverns, trying to keep contact with the men on either side of me, racing toward every suspicious hummock or mound of sand, I calculated quickly in my mind: If the search circle spread a half mile in each direction, the two hundred and eighty-odd of us would be spread around a perimeter of nearly seventeen thousand feet . . . say, sixty feet between men all around the circle. Could one man search a strip sixty feet wide? I doubted it, worriedly; and worse, it was certain that even the giant flares from the whaleboats could not illuminate so vast an area. Long before we reached the half-mile mark, we would be relying on the comparatively feeble light of our headlamps.

We pushed on to the half-mile mark . . . and beyond.

We searched to the limit of our air supply before the recall signal, dimmed by distance, came faintly to our ears. Dejectedly we rose to the surface, stripped off our face masks and swam back to the whaleboats. There was almost absolute silence from the boats as the motors putt-putted us back to the wharf.

We were a defeated lot as we fell into formation at the wharfside, took a rollcall and were dismissed. The empty echo that came back when Eskow's name was called was accusing.

Several of my classmates fell in with me on the way back to quarters with words of sympathy. But what they said seemed hardly to penetrate; I simply could not believe that Bob Eskow was missing.

It was after midnight. We turned in at once—reveille was canceled for the morning after a night exercise, but still we would have to be up by seven to begin classes. I lay in my unbelievably empty room, staring at the dark ceiling, trying to understand what had happened. It was impossible. He had been there with me; and then he wasn't.

I must have lain awake for hours, staring into the darkness.

But sometime I must have fallen asleep, for the next thing I knew someone was shaking my shoulder. "Eden!" came Lt. Hachette's excited voice. "Eden! They found him—he's alive!"

I struggled to my feet. "What?" I demanded, hardly believing.

"It's true!" Hachette said. "He was picked up by a fishing boat, three miles from the drop point. Heaven knows how he got there—but he's alive!"

Alive he was; but that was all we knew. There was an official announcement at morning mess: "Cadet Eskow has been rescued by a small Bermudan vessel and taken to a civilian hospital. He is in fair condition, but will require hospitalization for some time." And a few days later I got a letter from Bob in the hospital; but it had few more details. It was a seven days' wonder at the Academy: How had he got there? What had happened? But all we had were the questions, no answers, and as the days and weeks passed Bob's name became less and less likely to crop up.

It was, in a way, a difficult time for me. At the Academy the "buddy' principle was strongly in force; you and your roommate were supposed to work with each other, look out for each other, know at all times where the other person was. If Bob Eskow had been removed from the Academy duty lists I would have had another roommate assigned me—someone whose original roommate had washed out, perhaps; but he was only on sick leave and his room was kept open for him.

It was more than a little lonely. What made the time not only tolerable but fast-flying was, first, the heavy work schedule—we were all far too busy to brood. And, second, there were the letters from my uncle.

There was no telling when one would arrive; I had gone months on end without hearing from him, then suddenly I would get nearly a letter a day, scarlet ink on stiff yellow paper, sometimes short, sometimes marvelously long. Reading my uncle Stewart's letters was almost like taking the long, deep trip to Marinia; through them I saw the sights and wonders of the watery world he inhabited, which I hoped to make my own. I could almost see him before me as I read, tall, tanned to a dark leathery brown by the violet light of the sub-tea Troyon Tubes, chin fringed with that bronze beard. I could almost hear his soft, whispering voice telling me of the new world waiting.

Almost as real to me as the sun-drenched Academy grounds outside my window were the great sub-sea cities he wrote of—Thetis, Nereus, Seven Dome, Black Camp and the others—secure on the deep Pacific bed under their domes of the Edenite he had invented. For Uncle Stewart was a man of many enterprises. In the years since I had seen him I had begun to learn a few of them—not from his letters, for he spoke always of what I would do in Marinia, seldom of himself—but from the books and newspapers I devoured. I heard of him boring for petroleum in the new fields two miles down; of the platinum prospect he had staked out in the submarine range called Moutains of Darkness because its rugged slopes are bare of the phosphorescent life that much of the sea-mountains show; of my uncle in a thousand ventures, knocking about the floor of the Pacific from the Kermadec Deep to the Tuscarora.

If I had stopped to think, I might have found myself asking many questions. Petroleum, platinum and other ores; rare deep-sea creatures whose dead carcasses provided the raw materials for astonishing new drugs; his royalties (I didn't know then that he had never been able to collect them) on the Edenite process itself . . . my uncle should have been a multi-millionaire many times over. But he never mentioned money, and never seemed like a man of wealth.

Hc also never mentioned Hallam Sperry, the father of my executive officer.

Significant gaps! I could scarcely have guessed how closely they were connected!

I had not realized how important Bob Eskow was to me until he was away. I kept in touch with the hospital, but it was a complete surprise, all the same, when one of our classmates hailed me as we returned from the evening meal to say that Bob was back.

I raced into Fletcher Hall and into the elevator, grinning all over, oblivious to everything else as I punched the button for my floor.

A little too oblivious, maybe. "Mis-ter Lubber!" crackled a familiar voice, and I leaped to attention. It was Cadet Captain Brand Sperry, standing arms akimbo outside the elevator. The door started to close, and hastily I punched the *Stop* button. Sperry's whiplash voice snapped: "Stand at attention, Mr. Lubber!"

"Yes, sir," I said.

"The Orders of the Day, Mr. Eden," he said sharply. "Have you had an opportunity to read them?"

"Yes, sir." I knew what was coming.

"Oh?" He affected to look surprised. He shook his head. "I cannot understand that, Mr. Eden. It is very prominently posted on the bulletin board—I can see it from here—that from 0600 this day onward until further notice, elevators will not be used. That is a general order, Mr. Eden, put forth by higher authority in an effort to conserve power. Or weren't you aware that there is a power shortage? Uranium is in short supply, Mr. Eden; without uranium, power must be conserved. Do you understand that?"

"Yes, sir." It went on from there; it wound up with an order to spend the next day's half-hour before-dinner rest period at attention in front of the bulletin board, memorizing the orders of the day. I could stand that well enough; what hurt was that Cadet Captain Sperry had been within easy earshot when the classmate had called to me that Eskow was back in our room. He knew why I had been hurrying, and why I was absent-minded.

He knew, and yet he jumped on me for what was, after all, the smallest of offenses. I was finding it very difficult to live under the rule of Cadet Captain Brand Sperry.

But five minutes later, in our room, Bob Eskow made up for much.

I pumped his hand in a storm of warm feeling. "Bob!" I said, inarticulately. "I never expected to see you again!"

His grin wavered. In a dour tone, he said: "You may not see me for very long, at that. I'm on probation."

"Probation! But—"

He shrugged. "They're right, in a way," he said. "Wait a minute, and I'll tell you everything that happened. Back at the night maneuver, I went down for the exercises right behind you and we all started off for the defensive line. I remember turning my headlamp off. And I remember wondering how in the world I could tell if I was swimming up, down, sidewise or what. Then—" he hesitated and shook his head— "then something happened, Jim. I don't honestly know exactly what. The doctor said something about abnormal sensitivity to pressure and blacking out—I don't know. All I know is, all of a sudden, everything got foggy. I couldn't seem to get my breath, and things were getting black—although everything was so black to start out with that it was kind of hard to tell. Then—" he spread his hands— "then I was on the deck of a little fishing ketch; they'd pulled me up in the nets."

I said, "But, Bob—"

"I know," he said. "I'd been in the water for a long time—I was just about out of oxygen, they told me. But I was alive. They didn't have any radio in the ketch, and they didn't see why they should be bothered bringing me in to the Academy wharf, so they took be to their home port. And then they phoned the Academy, and a Regular medical officer from the Sub-Sea Base came down and got me—and there I was, in the hospital."

"But what knocked you out?"

He looked at me somberly. "The medical officer asked me a lot of silly questions about that. First he thought it was a malfunction of the breathing apparatus, but then he got an engineering report that wrecked that idea. So he just patted me on the head and told me some people were more susceptible to these things than others and, after all, I could have a perfectly good life as a lubber civilian. . . ."

I gaped at him. "Bob, you're not *washed out?*"

He grinned and poked me on the shoulder—but the grin wasn't as happy as it could have been. "Not quite," he said. "Not quite, but it was pretty close. They had a hearing, right there in the hospital, as soon as I was able to sit up and take notice. And I managed to convince them that, after all, it *might* have been malfunction of the apparatus, so they allowed as how they might give me another chance. But—well, it's on my record, Jim. It isn't any disgrace to get washed out of the Academy for medical reasons, I know that—but I don't want to get washed out for *any* reason. Any little thing now—anything that might ordinarily get me a hard time from the Commandant, for instance—and I'm out."

I said indignantly, "Bob, there's been some kind of mistake. That's not fair! Maybe it *was* punk equipment— they can't put that kind of a mark on your record unless they're *sure*. Did they take into consideration your record here? All the calisthenics, and the other underwater exercises, and—"

He wasn't smiling at all now. He said soberly, "They sure did, Jim. You might say that was the biggest part of it. They had sworn evidence that, from my first day at the Academy, I had been consistently showing signs of being unable to keep up with the rest of the class—puffing and panting and not quite making the number of pushups and so on."

I was aghast. "But—"

"But nothing! That's the story, Jim. I won't deny that maybe I haven't got as many muscles as you do—who does? But I think I've held my end up in everything we did. Only—the testimony said different."

"*What* testimony?" I demanded. "Who told them a cock-and-bull story like that?"

"He made it mighty plausible, Jim," Bob said gently. "It was a good friend of yours. He showed up right at the hospital, and he was just the model of a perfect sub-sea cadet while he was answering questions. You know who I mean—Cadet Captain Brand Sperry, himself."

6

The Cruise of the *Pocatello*

My second summer at the Academy I almost saw my Uncle Stewart.

I had come a long way from the clumsy young civilian who had entered the Academy's coral gates two years before. We all had. Two solid years of drill, work and study had turned us into—well, not real sub-sea officers; not yet. But certainly something as far removed from our soft civilian days as possible. I could skin-dive to forty feet, lung-dive to seven hundred, suit-dive to limits of the Edenite armor's capacity. I could name the duties of every crewman on any fighting sub-sea vessel of the service; in a pinch, I could take those duties over—from scrambling eggs for eight hundred men in the galley to conning my ship through a delicate harbor approach.

True, it was all book-learning, or nearly all. I had yet to put most of my new skills into practice; and I had a good two years more of advanced studies ahead of me before I could be commissioned. But it was as a sea-faring man, a certified midshipman of the Sub-Sea Service, and not as a lubber that, with the rest of my class—now less than two hundred strong—I embarked for our round-the-world training cruise on the old *SSS Pocatello*.

It was to be a ninety-day cruise, across the North

Atlantic, through the Mediterranean and the Suez Canal, through the Red Sea to the Gulf of Aden, where we would take part in Fleet Exercises; then across the Indian Ocean and the treacherous waters around the East Indies to Marinia. There, I hoped, I would have a liberty and a chance to see my uncle again, before we began the long cross-Pacific leg to the Panama Canal and thence back to our Caribbean base. We had just over thirty thousand miles to go, almost all of it submerged; only at Suez and Panama would *Pocatello* transit the canals as a surface vessel.

The crossing of the Atlantic was child's play. I suppose we needed it to break into the routine of sub-ship life; but there was almost nothing for us to do but stand our watches, keep our engines going and wait until the slow eight-day crossing was over. We ran the ship; there was a skeleton complement of Regulars aboard, but their job was only to stand by in case of disaster, and to observe and make reports on us.

Pocatello's Second Officer was Cadet Captain Sperry. He was not technically in command, but he had the functions of an exec; and there was enough of a component of command in his post to give Bob Eskow and me uneasy moments. But there was no trouble all the way across the Atlantic.

We drifted in through the Gates of Hercules—the Straits between Gibraltar and the African shore—with our engines stilled, a trick the ancient Diesel-powered submarines used to use in wartime so that they could steal through the narrow passage unchallenged. The shallow Mediterranean is a giant evaporating pan; water is sucked in from the Atlantic continually. Under the hot Mediterranean sun some of the water steams off and a dense salt solution remains; it sinks to the bottom and flows out again through the Straits of Gibraltar—a dense, heavy outgoing current flowing under a fresher, lighter incoming current, never ending, never mixing. We rode in on the upper current but still well below the surface. I was on the bridge, scanning the waters around us through the microsonar as we transited the Straits; it was an eerie sensation to be there in that big old war vessel, the engines dead and the helm unresponsive, and to see the check points in the sonar screen drift by.

"Well done," said the Regular officer who was standing by, closing his notebook with a snap. "You may take the conn and surface, Cadet Captain Sperry."

We set course for the fueling base at the Rock itself—not because we needed fuel but because new orders had come through requiring it. There was no explanation of the orders—but a lot of gossip. We listened to all the gossip, Bob and I, and agreed to discount it—which was a mistake, in a way. Because on the same principle as that of the broken clock, which tells the right time twice a day, of all the contradictory explanations the scuttlebutt gave for our new orders, some of them turned out to be right.

We came into the great U.N. refueling base in broad daylight and on the surface. My relief came before we moored, but I was reluctant to go off duty; Bob Eskow, relieved at the same time from his duties as Junior Engineering Officer, turned up in our wardroom and the two of us slipped silently up to the weather deck, staying as much out of sight as we could. There was no reason we shouldn't be there—the ship was secured against diving—but neither one of us wanted any of Cadet Captain Sperry's caustic tongue right at that moment.

We looked at the enormous limestone cliff in wonderment. "We're bound to get liberty," said Bob happily. "This ought to be good, Jim! We'll climb up and see the Barbary apes and look across the Straits at Mount Abyla. And there's a cave—St. Michael's, the name is—that some people say goes all the way under the water to Africa, and—"

"Attention on deck," rasped a loudspeaker behind us. "You two cadets on the weather deck. Report to the O.O.D.—you're both on report!"

We came to crisp attention as the commander's voice snapped at us. On report! We saluted the bridge and went below, a lot less cheerful than we had been a moment before.

"There goes your climb to see the apes," I grumbled to Bob at the gangway. "Of all the rotten luck—"

His face was grim. He nudged me and nodded at the bridge. "It wasn't luck, Jim," he said. "I doubt the commander would have bothered us, even if we weren't supposed to be there. But—take a look."

I glanced up. There on the weather bridge stood the commander, no longer looking at us, carefully supervising the mooring operation. But beside him, and looking our way with a particularly pleased expression, was our Second Officer, Cadet Captain Sperry.

Instead of a liberty at Gibraltar, we spent our off-duty time in port doing pushups in the training area at the fueling base. It wasn't too bad—ten minutes of calisthenics, and a five-minute break; for two hours at a time. But in one of the breaks Bob spotted something that neither one of us could figure out.

The loading machines were active around the *Pocatello*—which was normal enough; you expect to see a ship fueled at a fueling station, and the spaced piles of uranium slugs that the machine was working on, each in its own little radiation-proof can, didn't attract our attention at first.

Until Bob noticed that the slugs were coming *off* the ship.

"Unloading fuel!" I said, unbelieving. "But that's crazy—we've got thirty thousand miles to go."

Bob wiped his brow, panting—he took the exercises harder than I did. He shook his head. "We don't need it," he said slowly. "One fuel load would carry this tub around the world two or three times, easily enough. That's just our emergency reserve. But it's funny, all the same."

We agreed it was funny, and then the whistle blew and the dozen or so of us who were working off demerits began our pushups again. But we forgot it—for a while.

By nightfall *Pocatello* was on her way again, to the

naval base at Naples. It was an uneventful voyage. We surfaced just outside the Gulf of Naples, and rode in between the twin islands of Ischia and Capri just at sunrise. I had the morning watch, and I saw the sun come up over the gently steaming cone of Vesuvius.

It was there that we got the bad news:

The cruise was called off.

Officially, there was no reason given; simply a terse mailgram order for *Pocatello* to return to base. But the scuttlebutt had the explanation, and remembering what Bob and I had seen at Gibraltar I couldn't doubt that it was true:

Uranium shortage.

I don't suppose there was a man on the ship who didn't take it hard when the word got out—all of us had looked forward to that training cruise for a long time. But to me it meant losing something more than a pleasure trip. I had been looking forward, more than I realized, to the chance of being in Marinia, and seeing my uncle, Stewart Eden.

Well, that was out, for now.

It was early morning when the orders came to return to Bermuda. *Pocatello* was being provisioned, and couldn't be ready to leave before night. Bob Eskow and I had liberty for the afternoon, but we were in pretty dismal spirits in the whaleboat.

But our spirits lifted once we were ashore. Neither of us had ever been so far from home; Naples seemed like another world to us, as remote from my New London and Bob's New York as the moon.

We toured the ancient, narrow streets, walked along the broad boulevard at the water's edge, stopped for strong, thick coffee in a glass-roofed *galleria* in the heart of the city.

As we sat drinking our coffee, a slim, dark-featured man with a warm smile came over to us. "*Scusi, signori,*" he said. He wore a sea-blue uniform with the fouled anchors of the Italian Sub-Sea command. Bob and I stood up hesitantly. I said:

"Hello. We—we don't speak Italian, sir."

The man shrugged. "Perhaps I speak a little of En-

glish," he said, slowly but with very little accent. "I pray
that you excuse me for interrupting, but you are of the
submarine American, are you not?"

"Why, yes," Bob said, grinning. "I'm Sub-Sea Cadet
Eskow, and this is Cadet Eden." He stuck out his hand.
The Italian took it, beaming.

"I knew!" he said. "Permit me to welcome you to
Napoli, gentlemen. I am Sotto-tenente Vittorio di
Laterani, at your service."

Both Bob and I realized at the same moment that we
were talking to a commissioned officer; we stumbled and
flustered and made quick salutes. He returned the salutes
with profound courtesy; he expressed his pleasure at the
presence of our ship in the harbor, and offered us his serv-
ices as guide for the remainder of the afternoon.

Bob and I looked at each other. We didn't have to say
a word; we both were delighted with the offer.

Lieutenant di Laterani was very little older than Bob
and myself; he was just twenty, and had been commissioned only the year before. He was attached to the
Naples base for the time being, his own sub-sea cruiser—
the *Pontevecchio*—having been drydocked for major
overhaul. His time was pretty much his own until the
overhaul was completed; when he suggested that he get
his car and take us on a tour of the Base, we were only
too quick to accept.

It was a wonderful afternoon. But it had a dismal
ending.

The clouds had been piling up around Mt. Vesuvius all
through the afternoon. Even now, I can hardly bear to
remember it: We were in a tiny hotel on the side of Mt.
Vesuvius for one last *cafe-espresso* and a look at the Gulf
of Naples when the storm struck.

Tenente di Laterani leaped to his feet at the first rum-
ble of thunder. *"Madre mio!"* he cried. "Come, gentlemen—let us hurry. The road down the mountain, it is
impassable when the rain is heavy. And if you must make
your sailing——"

We didn't make it.

We got to the dock where *Pocatello* had tied up less than an hour after sundown; but it might as well have been a year. *Pocatello* was gone.

We tried everything. The *tenente*, covered with shame because he had made us miss our ship, roared with us in his tiny automobile to the Base Headquarters and set about getting us transportation—torpedo boats, aircraft, anything that would get us to *Pocatello* before she got clear of the land and submerged for the long cruise back. But the storm had grounded the aircraft; and by the time di Laterani had wheedled the torpedo-boat commander into agreeing to take us to the ship, the Base radar shack sent over a visual: "American sub-sea cruiser submerged and out of recall range."

We had missed our ship.

The only thing to do was to report to the American section officer and take our medicine.

It was bitter medicine to take.

I think it would have been all right, under the circumstances, if we had been able to rejoin *Pocatello* even at Gibraltar. But it was not to be. The section officer took pity on us and radioed *Pocatello* our story, with a plea to surface at Gibraltar so that we could fly there and rejoin the craft. It seemed hours before the answer came back:

Request denied. Subject cadets will return to Academy by air.

Brand Sperry, Second Officer
Acting Commander

The next morning we boarded a commercial jet liner for the long, dreary trip back.

When we arrived at the Academy, we met with a flint-faced reception. The commandant himself called us in. We were a disgrace to the service, he said; Eskow's accident of his first year now seemed, in the light of this new happening, to have been deliberate; I, he said, had been trading on my uncle's and father's illustrious reputation. We were given our choice: Resign from the service, or face a court-martial.

I think that my father would have taken the court-martial. But it would have done no good for Eskow to refuse to resign; in view of his first accident, the court was sure to find against him. And I could not accept the possibility of myself staying in the service while Eskow, for the identical fault, was dismissed without honor.

We resigned.

It did not occur to me, even then, that something more than mere discipline was behind our difficulties.

With a heavy heart I sent my uncle a long radiogram to tell him what had happened, and began to pack my bags.

7

The Letter from the Deeps

When the answer came, it was simply a radiogram:

ACKNOWLEDGE. CHIN UP. LETTER FOLLOWS. STEWART EDEN.

The letter took a week to follow.

I wish it had been forever.

It was an unfamiliar long, blue envelope, and in the upper left hand corner was the name and address of my uncle's attorney. When I ripped it open, three things fell out. A check, for an amount that made my eyes bulge. A narrow yellow card, with my uncle's scrawl in scarlet: "Don't worry, Jim. I should have expected this; it isn't your fault. Come to Thetis. I'll meet you and explain."

It was a cryptic note; I read it twice, trying to decide what my uncle had meant. Did he mean he expected me to fail the difficult course? But that didn't square with "it isn't your fault." Bothered, I turned to the last enclosure.

And I at once forgot the others. It was a letter, precisely typed on tough blue cellutane, beneath a letterhead that said "Wallace Faulkner, Attorney at Law":

Mr. James Eden
Courtesy of United States Sub-Sea Academy
Class Three, Crew Five

Dear Sir:

I regret to inform you that your uncle, Stewart Eden, is dead. Shortly after writing you the enclosed note he embarked on a cruise to Seven Dome. The route from Thetis to Seven Dome passes over the Eden Deep; while crossing this deep, cruising at four thousand fathoms and on course, your uncle's ship was heard to transmit what seemed to be the beginning of distress signal. It was cut off in the middle; and no further contact was made.

The local naval authorities of course made every effort to contact your uncle, but without success. I am advised that there is no possibility that he has survived.

I suppose you are aware that you are the sole heir. I must warn you, however, that your uncle was not a very wealthy man.

The bulk of his estate comprises eighty shares of stock in a corporation known as Marine Mines, Ltd. This is a majority interest, since the corporation issued only one hundred shares. The value of these shares is problematical. Their par value is listed at one thousand dollars, but there is no market for them under ordinary conditions.

Some years ago this corporation filed with the government of Marinia a claim for the exploitation of Eden Deep, giving it full and sole surface and mineral rights. This is the major asset of the firm. While it may well be that the bottom underlying Eden Deep contains mineral deposits of great value, the difficulty of working them is apparent, since existing forms of seacars and sub-sea armor have not been used successfully at any such depths. It is possible that your uncle's death, indeed, may be due to an attempt to extend the downward range of his equipment sufficiently to exploit the bottom of Eden Deep. If so, the attempt was of course unsuccessful.

To put it plainly, the project of mining this claim is visionary and impractical. Apart from the difficulties imposed by the crushing pressure of thousands of fathoms of water, the Deep is inhabited by many dangerous sea creatures, including benthoctopus and the almost unknown animal called K'Wapti. It is even reputed to be the den of the fabulous sea-serpent, though this is of course speculative.

Fortunately for your interests, however, I have among my clients a person who is willing to invest in this property as a speculation, in the faint possibility that new techniques may make it possible to exploit its presumable resources. There are, as you perhaps know, no such new techniques in sight. Moreover, you may be aware that under Marinian maritime law, claims must be proved within eight years or they revert to the public domain. That is, actual mining operations must begin within that period.

The eight-year period ends on February 1st of next year. You will realize that, even should some new techniques be developed, there would not remain sufficient time to put them to use before the claim expired.

For this reason, I earnestly advise you to accept any offer that may be made for this property. I am authorized to offer you four hundred dollars a share for this block of eighty shares of Marine Mines Ltd., making a total of thirty-two thousand dollars.

There is no possibility that this price can be exceeded.

Please inform me by radio of your acceptance of this offer at once. I have already drawn up the necessary contract of sale and will proceed to execute it as soon as I have your authorization. My client may withdraw the offer at any time, so haste is absolutely essential. I assure you that the stock would not command a fraction of this price in the open market.

The remainder of your uncle's estate comprises the seacar in which he was lost, which is extremely unlikely to be salvaged, and a few personal items, which are being sent you by sub-sea mail.

You may trust me to care for your interests as zealously as I have those of your uncle.

I shall await your radiogram authorizing me to proceed with the sale of the stock.

With deepest solicitude for you in your affliction,

I remain, faithfully your servant,

Wallace Faulkner

8

The Man in the White Suit

The death of Uncle Stewart was a painful shock to me—
all the more since it followed so brutally fast on the heels
of my forced resignation from the Academy. But I almost
forgot my personal troubles when I read Faulkner's letter,
with its accompanying aching sense of loss. If only I had
been able to complete the cruise, I thought; if only we had
gone through the plan as scheduled, and I had seen him
in Marinia. . . .

But there was no point in wasting tears over what was
too late to mend. I talked it over with Bob Eskow, in
New York, where I had flown from the Academy. He
agreed with me that Faulkner's letter raised as many
questions as it answered, that perhaps I should not be too
quick to accept the offer his unnamed client had made.
But that meant so little to me, in comparison with the
personal loss of my uncle, my last living relative.

For so many years I had been looking forward to
exploring the wonders of Marinia in his company! The
Sub-Sea Service would surely have based me near there;
we would have been able to see each other often, to do so
many things together.

It seemed incredible that he could be dead.

I decided to go to Marinia at once, to see if anything

could yet be done to find my uncle's body, then to take charge of the mining proposition in Eden Deep. "Impossible?" I hardly knew the word. After all, I was just seventeen!

I sent Faulkner a radiogram telling him that the shares of Marine Mines were not for sale, and that I was coming to Thetis at once, to claim the legacy.

His reply was immediate:

NOT NECESSARY FOR YOU TO COME TO THETIS. I WILL CARE FOR YOUR INTERESTS. MY ADVICE TO SELL SHARES AT ONCE. AM AUTHORIZED TO OFFER PAR VALUE FOR MY CLIENT. TOTAL PRICE THEREFORE EIGHTY THOUSAND DOLLARS. RADIO ACCEPTANCE IMMEDIATELY. TRUST ME.

WALLACE FAULKNER.

That was an exciting message. I showed it to Bob and he agreed. Strange that the unknown person who had so "reluctantly" made the offer of thirty-two thousand dollars should so quickly and easily more than double it!

If it were worth so much to him, it should be valuable to me too. And I felt a vague distrust of Faulkner. If my uncle used him he must be honest, certainly. Still. . . .

His protestations were hard to take. Too much talk of "trust" and "solicitude"; too few explanations. Why had he been in such a hurry for me to sell at thirty-two thousand dollars when, a matter of days later, he could get an offer of eighty?

Bob Eskow said it: "I don't know whether he's a crook or a bum businessman. Either way, I'd watch him!"

I replied:

SHARES NOT FOR SALE, ARRIVING ON ISLE OF SPAIN.

And I caught a jet transport to San Francisco to make contact with the giant submarine liner there.

I landed at the San Francisco harbor jet-field in a fog.

I had just time to confirm my reservations on the sub-sea liner, *Isle of Spain*, get my passport and spend a few hours sight-seeing. The liner was to sail direct for Marinia; it was one of the finest vessels in the Pacific submarine service, and I looked forward to the trip with real joy and excitement. How quickly one can forget! It was not yet a week since I had learned of Uncle Stewart's death, only two weeks and a bit since I had suffered the worst disgrace imaginable by being asked to resign from the Academy—but I was already looking forward to adventure. I might as well admit that I was looking forward, too, to being taken seriously by Wallace Faulkner and the others at Thetis. After all, I would be the sole owner of a controlling interest in a corporation! True, the corporation might be as worthless as Faulkner indicated.

But I refused to believe that. As I say, I was only seventeen.

I wondered a bit who my unknown partner—the owner of the remaining twenty per cent of the stock—might be. Uncle Stewart had said nothing; and Faulkner had been bafflingly silent.

But all those questions would be answered in time. . . .

I got my passport with no difficulty; since Marinia had become an independent nation under the United Nations trusteeship, many Americans went there as a matter of course, for vacations, for business or just for the trip. The *Isle of Spain* would have a large passenger list of vacationers, I knew; it would touch at Black Camp and little Eden Dome before going on to Thetis. With my passport I gathered together my I.D. card—actually, it was a booklet with my whole life's history in it—from the Academy, and my birth certificate; I didn't know what papers I would need to establish my identity as Stewart Eden's heir, and I didn't want to be caught short. I packed a small bag; the rest of my belongings I checked in the hotel baggage room.

The desk clerk had another radiogram for me, forwarded from New York:

YOUR COMING TO MARINIA UNNECESSARY
AND UNWISE. IMPOSSBLE FOR YOU TO WORK
MINING CONCESSION. I WARN YOU IT IS FOOL-
ISH AND SUICIDAL. MY CLIENT MAKES FINAL
OFFER OF TWICE PAR VALUE FOR SHARES.
MUST BE ACCEPTED BY RETURN RADIO. POSI-
TIVELY CAN SECURE NO BETTER BID.
                              WALLACE FAULKNER

A hundred and sixty thousand dollars!

I began to feel rich.

If anything had been needed to make me more anxious
to get to Thetis at once—and more determined to turn
down any offer that might come along—this was it. Why
was Faulkner so anxious for me to stay away? What was
his reason for harping on the "danger" in Eden Deep?

I repeated my previous radio.

And then, to add my confusion, I discovered I was
being followed.

I was on my way downtown, riding the railed passenger express belt, on my way to the Ferry Building.

It was a chill, gloomy day, a dense sea-fog hanging
over the city. Though it was still afternoon, the lights
were on, gleaming red circles of yellow mist. The
beacons from the jet port shone through the cold gray
only dimly; the scarlet fog-lights on the low-flying heli-
copters used for suburban transit were moving red blurs
in the gloom.

Coat buttoned high against the misty wind, I stood on
the vibrating belt, leaning against a hand-rail, thinking of
the trip before me. Quite by accident I noticed a big man
lounging on the belt fifty yards behind me. I might have
ignored him, but there was something vaguely unhealthy
about him; soft, heavy, out of condition. He was dressed
carelessly and in bad taste, I thought: White tunic and
trousers, close fitting and a little soiled. A long blue cloak;
a black cane with a silver head; a wide, high-crowned red
felt sombrero on his head.

He looked somewhat familiar, in the way that a

stranger sometimes does. I thought I had seen him before quite casually, it seemed to me; but I couldn't quite pin down where.

Then I reached my stop on the express belt and got off, dismissing him from my mind. ...

But not for long.

At the Ferry Building I joined the line at the sub-ship reservations desk and claimed my stateroom on the *Isle of Spain*. When I turned away with the confirmation in my hand, I saw that the man in white had been right behind me.

That was no coincidence!

I was certain of it; but I could prove it beyond any question of doubt if I chose. I made the effort.

The man did not appear to be paying any attention to me. He asked some sort of question of the clerk at the desk and got a short answer; whereupon he nodded and drifted over to a side of the room, staring thoughtfully out the window. His eyes were hidden beneath the broad red brim of his hat; white-gloved fingers were tapping on the window ledge.

But I was morally sure he saw every move I made.

I bought a newstape at the stand in the Ferry Building, and strode out the door. There was no looking back, either the man followed me, or he did not.

I headed down toward the water, walking at a brisk pace. It was now full dark; I had a few hours yet before the *Isle of Spain*'s sailing at midnight, but little time to waste. The sky was a dome of dull yellow light, the city's lights reflected back from the blanket of fog. Bright, hazy haloes clung to street lamps and beacons. All to the good!

I swung around a dark corner in an almost deserted street, near the docks that once had been so tumultuously busy night and day and now were nearly abandoned, and ducked into a doorway.

The man in the white suit fell neatly into the trap. He came quietly around the corner; I didn't hear him until he was almost before my doorway. I stepped out, hand in my pocket to make it look as though I had a gun, and said:

"Hold it!"

He showed no surprise. He stared at me from under the red brim for a moment. Then he said evenly, "Don't shoot."

His breathing was slow; he was not at all excited. For a moment the thought had crossed my mind: Suppose I was wrong? Suppose he was a harmless pedestrian—suppose he cried out and the police came? The natural presumption would be that I was a hold-up man; no doubt I could clear myself, but I certainly would miss my ship—and one experience of missing a ship was enough for me!

But this man was no harmless pedestrian. It was almost as though he expected trouble. He didn't move a muscle as he said: "Take it easy, boy. Careful with the gun."

"Careful!" I said angrily. "What are you following me for? Hurry up—talk!"

He said with mock-innocence, "What in the world are you talking about?"

I said hotly, "You know! Don't waste my time—come across or I'll shoot!"

Naturally, I had no intention of shooting—even if I had had a gun to shoot with! Whether he knew that I will never know; he turned to face me more squarely, moved his lips as though he were about to speak. His mouth opened a little. . . .

Too late I saw the tiny, glittering metal thing he held between his teeth.

The tiny stream had already jetted from it as he crushed it between his teeth, forced the spurt of its contents. I felt the cold little drops strike my cheek. Instantly the chillness changed to a stabbing sensation of heat. Searing flame flashed over the side of my face; hot needles stabbed into my brain.

I should have known, I told myself dazedly in that split-second of realization—I should have known he would protect himself. The anesthetic-capsule was an old trick; I should have thought of it. . . .

Sheets of blinding light were flickering before my sight. They faded.

Then there was only darkness. I felt myself falling as the anesthetic struck home.

It must have been an hour or more before I came to.

I got stiffly to my feet, muscles aching from the damp ground.

I was in the doorway still; no one was in sight. Leaning against the wall for support, I took quick inventory of my pockets.

I had been searched; that much was obvious. My wallet was on the ground, my passport hanging half out of it.

But nothing seemed to be missing. Not my passport; not my I.D. card; not my money or my watch. It had been no simple robbery, that was certain; I carried quite a lot of money, and not a penny of it was gone.

I tried to brush off my sodden clothing and staggered to the corner. I had no idea of the time; all I could think of was the sailing of the *Isle of Spain* at midnight.

Luck was with me. An empty cab cruised by overhead; I hailed it, and it settled to the curb beside me with a gentle whir of its rotor blades.

I thought briefly of the police; certainly I should report this. . . .

But, by the dashboard clock in the helicab, I had just time to make the sailing.

I ordered the cab pilot to take me to the slip where the *Isle of Spain* was waiting. Fortunately my bags were already aboard; nothing, at any rate, had been lost by my unfortunate encounter with White Suit.

At least, that is what I thought at the time. . . .

9

Aboard the *Isle of Spain*

But when I boarded the *Isle of Spain* I forgot all my troubles.

The giant sub-sea liner, more than a thousand feet long, as thick through as a seven-story building, bobbed lightly in the Pacific swell. I boarded her through a covered ramp, but even so, through portholes in the ramp, I saw the gleaming Edenite armor that flanked her whole length, the mighty sweep of her lines, torpedo-shaped, forward and aft.

I was realizing one of the great ambitions of my life! Below this heaving, gray expanse lay the Pacific bottom, sloping off for miles in the shallow continental shelf, then plunging to the mighty Deeps where Marinia lay, three thousand miles away and fifteen hundred and more fathoms down.

In a matter of moments I would be slipping through the water, en route to the cities of the sea!

I almost forgot the Academy—my uncle's death—the man in the red hat.

Almost ... but not quite. I made a covert search of all the other passengers in sight. Vacationers, some of them, using the long sub-sea voyage as a pleasure cruise. Hard-bitten sub-sea miners, their skin dark in the Troyon light.

Keen-featured ship's officers and crew, moving efficiently through the crowds, getting ready to get under weigh. Even a group of ensigns and sub-lieutenants—I felt a sharp stab of jealousy—in the dress scarlet of the Sub-Sea Service.

But no one who looked at all dangerous to me; certainly no one as striking as the man in the red hat.

I signed on the passenger list, and waited for the steward to have me shown to my stateroom. I sat looking around at the passengers.

Then it occurred to me. The man in the red hat had been a striking figure; so conspicuous that he might almost be invisible through sheer obviousness, if I hadn't happened vaguely to recall seeing him.

Perhaps—perhaps whoever it was who was so interested in my doings would try the opposite tack. Perhaps someone so neutral and inconspicuous as to be even less visible would be next.

With new eyes I looked at the crowd in the saloon.

In a moment I had found him; I was sure of it.

He was slumped down, staring at the floor, in the midst of his luggage. A small man, thin, shrunken. His narrow face was expressionless; his pale eyes blank. His garments were a neutral gray, neither neat nor shabby.

He was the sort of individual who could enter a room without being noticed, who had no single characteristic that would stick in the memory.

Of course—I told myself—I might be seeing ghosts.

He might be a perfectly harmless passenger. Perhaps no one on the ship was interested in me at all. Still—the persons who had gone to such lengths to knock me out and search me on the deserted San Francisco streets would likely keep an eye on me still.

At any rate, I was going to keep an eye on him.

A white-clad steward came toward me; I handed my bags over to him, tipped him, and let him go to my stateroom without me. I accompanied him just as far as the entrance to the saloon; there I waited, out of sight, to see what the gray man would do.

In a few minutes he hailed a steward, handed over his bags, and moved off in the same direction as my own steward had gone. I let him get well ahead, then followed.

The steward led the thin little man past the elevator which communicated with the steerage quarters, past the moving stairs that went to the luxurious suites above. Good; his stateroom would be on the cabin deck, with mine.

The steward stopped to unlock a door; and he and the little man went in.

As soon as the steward had left and closed the door, I hurried past.

It was stateroom 335.

And my own stateroom was number 334.

I found a steward to make sure; he led me to the room next to the gray man's. He was going to be my next-door neighbor!

I no longer thought of coincidences. I knew!

The steward entered the stateroom behind me. He showed me how to adjust the Troyon light, how to regulate the gentle breeze of artificial air, how to work the temperature controls, the ship's radio, the washstands and equipment. Then he busied himself tidying the towels on their racks, in the ancient custom of his kind while waiting for a tip.

It *might* be an accident . . . but I knew it was not. The man in the red hat, after all, had had plenty of chance to find out my stateroom number—in the line behind me when I confirmed my reservation; or, if by any chance he had blundered enough to miss it then, when he went through my pockets later on. There could be no question that the gray man—assuming they worked together— could easily have arranged to get the stateroom next to mine.

But why?

I dug deep in my pocket to tip the steward.

He gave me a soft salute and started to leave. I stopped him.

"Say," I said carelessly, "do you know who's in the next cabin? I thought I recognized him as I came in."

He looked at me. "If you know him, sir, why not just——"

I added to the tip, and he gave me a different kind of look. "Can you find his name for me?"

The steward pursed his lips. "Certainly, sir. The passenger list will have it."

"Please do." He nodded, half winking, and left. Five minutes later he was at the door again. -

"The name is E. A. Smith, sir. No address." He hesitated. "Purser says it was a last-minute reservation," he added.

"Thanks," I said, trying to be nonchalant. "Guess I was wrong. There are lots of Smiths in the world."

"And a lot who aren't named Smith." He closed the door with a half smile.

When I came out of my cabin the next morning the ship was under weigh. I felt the slight roll of the vessel, not choppy like a surface ship, but gentle and soothing, as the ship slid through the strong undersea currents; that, and the almost imperceptible vibration of the screws, was the only signal that we were racing forward at sixty knots or better.

It was achingly familiar. . . .

I struck up a friendship with a junior officer after breakfast, and he offered to show me around the ship. I was delighted to take him up on it.

First we went to the narrow promenade around the cabin deck, just inside the hull. He opened a metal shutter inside a port and we looked out.

It was the sight I had seen so many times before: Darkness, and an occasional dimly luminous shape flashing past.

"We're a hundred fathoms down," the officer volunteered. "That water's ice-cold. Under a pressure close to a quarter-ton to the square inch."

I nodded. "I know," I said. I reached out and closed the port. He looked at me curiously, but said nothing.

We went below; he showed me the ballast tanks with their powerful pumps, the battery deck with its rows of

Vauclain cells in the unimaginable event of a failure of the power reactor. We skirted the giant bulk of the reactor itself, whispering songs of neutrons and fission in its gentle tones. We went through the engine rooms, clean and orderly, smelling slightly of lubricating oil. It was almost soundless, only the dull vibration of the screws and the windy sigh of the steam coming out of the turbines, at the end of the heat-exchanger chain.

We saw it all—cargo holds, forecastle, steerage, upper deck with its pool and conservatory, superstructure atop the hull with its pilot house, chart house, radio room, officer's quarters.

It was as different from the battered, cramped old *Pocatello* as an emerald is from mud.

But I knew which I would have chosen, had I had the choice.

The day passed. We ate; the afternoon drifted by; we ate again; the evening came. And the *Isle of Spain* lunged on through the submarine blackness.

It was growing late and I retired to my cabin.

Something was awry.

I stood on the threshold, key still in the door, listening and looking and waiting.

Through no sense that the doctors admit exists, I knew something had happened. The stateroom was not just as it had been when I left. Something had changed.

I switched on the Troyon tubes and looked around.

If there had been a search of my luggage, it had been unbelievably skillful. I could detect nothing that had been disturbed. But the feeling persisted.

I decided on an inch-by-inch examination of the cabin.

And in the bath, behind the towel rack, I found what I was looking for.

There was plaster dust on the floor beneath. And behind the rack itself, hidden by the bar on which the towels hung unless you looked just so, was a small round hole. It wasn't more than a quarter-inch in diameter, perhaps less; it had been drilled through the wall.

For what?

A fresh puzzle. I couldn't guess at the answer. Certainly it was not for spying—you couldn't see past the towel bar from the other side. For listening? Hardly; there were electronic devices that were much, much subtler and more reliable.

But certainly it was for something. . . .

If I couldn't figure out for what, at least I could take a sensible precaution. I called a steward, and told him I had decided to vacate the room.

If I had known what the consequences would be. . . .

But I didn't. How could I have guessed?

The steward looked dismayed when I told him what I wanted. "*Very* irregular, sir!" he sputtered. "Is the room unsatisfactory?"

It was not the same steward of the morning. I said, as haughtily as I could: "Steward, I want another room! That's all; get it for me, please. I understand that I shall have to pay for two rooms. I am quite prepared to do so."

It was a silly role to cast myself in; but the alternative was to tell him about the hole that had been drilled in the wall, and I wasn't quite ready to take anyone into my confidence.

He sputtered and sputtered some more; but I found a suitable bill in my pocket, and when it had been transferred to his he was much more co-operative. He shrugged. "This way, sir," he said, with the resignation one expects in those whose careers make them deal with many people. . . .

I slept like a baby that night. Soundly—

But by no means as soundly as I would have if I hadn't moved.

10

The Long Sleep

When I woke it took me a moment to realize where I was. My shaving gear, with everything else I owned, was still in Stateroom 334. I should have gone back for it; but the whisper of sound from the screws told me that something was happening; they were changed from the sounds of the day before.

I dressed quickly in the clothes I had worn and stepped out into the corridor. A passing crewman told me we were about to dock at Black Camp, first of the dome cities of Marinia. I would just have time for breakfast and a quick trip to the ship's barber for a shave.

I put off going back to my cabin.

The ship's barber tidied me up quickly; I left him feeling much improved, and headed for the dining salon.

On the way, I met the little man in gray.

For the first time he seemed actually to see me.

He stared at me unbelievingly with his pale eyes. He gasped; his thin-lipped mouth opened as if to speak. Every trace of color drained from his gray face.

He was trembling as, abruptly, he turned and fled.

One puzzle more. . . .

Why had he been so startled to see me? I couldn't guess; I dismissed the question, and went in to breakfast.

I had just finished eating when we docked at Black Camp—having made the run of two thousand miles and a bit in just over thirty-three hours. I hurried to the promenade, peered out through one of the shielded ports.

My first view of a city of the sea! Its weirdness and its wonder almost made me forget the web of mystery surrounding my life.

The vast, level plain of radiolarian ooze, shining with a cold, pale phosphorescence. Through some illusion of optics it seemed to stretch to infinity, though actually, owing to the turgidity of the water, the visibility was only a few hundred yards at best.

The "sky"—the cold ocean above us—was utterly black. Strange world: Luminous plains and glimmering mountains, under a black, black sky.

But all this was familiar to me. What was new was Black Camp itself, the huge hemispherical dome of Edenite that rose ghostly from the luminous plain. The massive bubble of metal armor that sheltered the city from the awful thrust of the sea.

The docking arrangement was the same as in all the deep-sea cities: tubes ran out from the city, under the rock of the sea-floor, the docks above them. The docks themselves were magnetic metal platforms, which the sub-sea vessel squats down to while a lock in her belly opens to join the tubes below.

From my stand on the promenade I could see only the featureless city dome and the unchanging sea; I wandered down to the saloon to watch the passengers disembark.

We took on a full score of passengers; at least as many got off.

And among those who got off was the gray man. He knew I was there; I caught one glimpse of his eyes on me out of the corner of mine, and in his I saw astonishment and what almost had to be fright. But then he looked at me no more. I stared after his departing back, wondering.

. . .

In a matter of minutes the locks were closed, the pressure-ports sealed, and the *Isle of Spain* was water-borne again.

I headed back toward my cabin. Since the little man was gone, there could be no reason to stay away. In fact, if I played my cards right—if the steward would let me in to Stateroom 335—I might learn something. . . .

I never got the chance.

Heedlessly I unlocked my stateroom door. Heedlessly I swung it open, started to step inside.

Bluish vapors swirled out upon me.

I staggered back, blinded, gasping, tears streaming down my face. I breathed the tiniest fraction of a minute whiff of the gases—and I was strangled, choking, bent double with a rasping, shattering cough.

Instantly a steward was by my side.

"Sir!" he cried. "Sir, what's the matter?"

Then he caught a whiff of the gas himself.

The two of us staggered away. He clawed at some sort of signal apparatus on the wall; in the distance, an alarm bell pulsed. A moment passed, then half a dozen crewmen appeared, in fire-fighting gear, masks and helmets giving them some protection. Without word or question they raced past us, heading from Stateroom 334. . . .

And in a moment two of them came lurching out. Between them they dragged a rigid, wax-faced form: the steward who had changed my cabin for me.

The captain of the *Isle of Spain* was considerate, tactful—and remorseless.

If I had had anything to hide, he would have had it from me. I was grateful that I could speak honestly to that bronze-faced man; I should not have cared to try him with a lie.

I told him everything. Starting with my forced resignation from the Academy—through the death of my uncle, the man in the red hat, the little gray man. I held nothing back.

I wanted to hold nothing back. I had got a quick glimpse of the unfortunate steward: grotesquely, frozenly stiff; hideously white—color bleached even from his hair and eyebrows by the searing action of the gas. The ship's doctor called the gas *lethine;* I had heard of it. It was deadly.

Whoever was behind the gray man was playing for keeps.

The ship's officers acted promptly; as soon as they had heard the first words of my story, they radioed Black Camp to have the gray man put under arrest. But I had small doubt that the gray man would be hard to find; certainly he knew what he would have to expect as soon as the corpse was discovered.

Unfortunate steward! The captain speculated that my story had interested him; he had gone back to Stateroom 334 to see just what it was that I was willing to pay double fare to get away from. And his curiosity had been his undoing.

Eventually the questioning was over. The captain secured my promise that, when I arrived at Thetis I would stay put until the Marinian police had had a chance to question me, if they wished to do so, and then I was at liberty.

I didn't go back to Stateroom 334. I had my belongings transferred to the new room. And I prayed that this last failure of my unknown enemies would exhaust their powers. . . .

We were due to arrive at Seven Dome late that night; I debated staying up for it, but decided not to bother. I was weary and worn; it had been a difficult period, and that day had been the most difficult of all.

I retired to my cabin rather early. But I didn't get a chance to go right to sleep.

There was a knock on my door. I flung it open; a steward smiled apologetically, and extended a scarlet envelope on a silver tray. "For you, Mr. Eden," he said. "Sorry to disturb you."

I dismissed him and ripped open the envelope. The message said:

Dear Mr. Eden:

I am sorry to hear of your difficulties. As you perhaps

know, your father, your uncle and I were once closely associated. Perhaps I can be of assistance to you.

Please come to my suite on A Deck when you receive this.

I stared at the note with the strangest mixed set of emotions I had ever known.

For the signature on the note was: "Hallam Sperry."

11

My Partner, My Enemy

Hallam Sperry himself admitted me to his cabin.

It was a far cry from the small stateroom I occupied on the deck below. It was more than a cabin, it was a suite; and properly so, I suppose. After all, *Isle of Spain* was only one of a dozen giant sub-sea liners on the Sperry Line! There were giant photomurals on the walls, pressure-tanks of curious deep-sea flower-animals and darting, tiny fish, tinted Troyon tubes to warm the rooms and give them the semblance of upper-air sunshine.

Hallam Sperry clasped my hand in a grip as sturdy and as cold as steel. He was a giant of a man, as big as my uncle had been but dark where Uncle Stewart had been fair, black-bearded where my uncle was ruddy. His eyes were a curious piercing blue; there was the coldness of the chill sea Deeps in those eyes as they looked into my mind. But there was a smile on his lips and his words were more than merely polite.

"Jim Eden," he rumbled. "Know a great deal about you, young man. Knew your father and his brother well— too bad about Stewart, but he was always a daredevil. Heard about your bad break at the Academy from my boy."

He offered me a spider-legged chair. What could I say

to the man? That the "bad break" at the Academy had been his son's own doing? That the struggle between him and the Edens was a public scandal?

I said nothing. We learned much at the Academy, but one of the first things we learned was not to speak until we knew what we had to say. It was possible that Hallam Sperry was not as black as he had been painted; it was not fair to attack him on the basis of rumor and old memories.

He offered me a crystal glass with a pale-green, stinging liquid in it; I tasted it and set it down—some strange liqueur from the Deeps. He said:

"An old friend of mine, Stewart Eden. Oh, we had our differences. But I always admired your uncle. Great man. Too bad he had to go like that."

I made some answer; but what I had to say made no difference. He rumbled right on, in his bass chiming voice. "Worked with Stewart for many years. Your father too. You'll hear stories about our fights—probably heard lots of them already. No matter, boy. He's gone now. Our differences are gone too. Question is, what next?"

I said, "I beg your pardon?"

"What next for you," he rumbled impatiently. "What are you going to do now? You're going to Thetis—why?"

I said stiffly, "I am my uncle's heir, Mr. Sperry. He left all of his interests to me."

"Interests!" Sperry snorted. "Guff! A bankrupt corporation and a sunk ship—I know what his 'interests' were." He looked at me piercingly. "You may not know this," he said. "Your uncle owed me money. Quite a lot. More than the value of his estate, boy."

I shifted uncomfortably. "I—I know nothing of that," I said. "Mr. Faulkner—Uncle Stewart's lawyer—didn't say anything about it."

"Course not. Faulkner didn't know. Gentlemen's agreement between your uncle and me; I loaned him the money, no note, nothing in writing. Question is, are you going to honor it."

I started to say something but he stopped me. "Belay that," he ordered. "Put it aside for a moment; business

can come later. Tell me first something about yourself."
He paused, and before I could speak the iron face
broadened into a smile. "And drink your drink," he
commanded. "That's an order, boy!"

I felt myself warming to the man; he had charm and a
hard-bitten strength that, to me, was greatly appealing.
Perhaps he was telling the truth; perhaps his bitter strug-
gles with my father and uncle were purely business trans-
actions, only the rough-and-tumble bouts of strong men
engaged in rivalry with each other. Certainly Hallam
Sperry had a warm smile and a strong handclasp. . . .

Still—I could not help but notice it: His lips smiled, but
his eyes were still sea-cold.

I told him about the Academy, my relations with his
son, Brand Sperry, the trouble in Italy and my forced
resignation. He was a receptive audience. I even found
myself telling him about the radiograms from Wallace Faulkner and my answers; even about the man in the
red hat and the little gray man and the *lethine* that had
murdered the steward, instead of me.

Careless of me. . . .

Still, I wonder. Hallam Sperry owned the *Isle of Spain*
and everything in it. Certainly he would know everything
that went on aboard it, in any case.

And I found out that he knew much, much more.

When I had finished my story he said, sipping his
sea-liqueur, "Bad breaks, boy. Question is, what do you
do now?"

I shook my head. "I don't know exactly, sir. I'm going
to Thetis. Then I'll look around and see what's what. I—I
don't know too much about Marinia, actually."

He gave a rumbling laugh. "Never thought I'd hear an
Eden admit that! Boy, Eden Dome is named after your
family!"

I said stiffly, "I know, sir. But after all, I've never been
here before. I don't even know what my uncle was doing
these last few years, as a matter of fact."

He looked surprised. "Oh, I can tell you that," he
offered. "Know everything that goes on in Marinia, I

don't mind admitting. Particularly about your Uncle Stewart, boy." He ticked off on his fingers. "First, platinum prospect in the Mountains of Darkness. Worked it for a year; then it petered out. Next, petroleum. Looked like a good bet; but your uncle sold out. Needed capital for something. For what? For Marine Mines Ltd. Sunk every nickel he had or could get his hands on into it. Finally sunk himself." He started to grin at his joke, but the expression on my face must have stopped him. "No offense, boy," he apologized. "Stewart was always a daredevil, you know."

"So you said," I answered.

He rolled on, "Come back to the main question. I staked your uncle last couple of years. Owes me money—more than half a million dollars. What are you going to do about it?"

"I don't know, sir," I admitted miserably. "This is the first I heard of it. I—I'll have to talk to Mr. Faulkner about that."

Hallam Sperry's expression changed curiously. For the first time, his face was in repose, but it was his eyes that were grinning at me—a faint, somehow alarming sardonic smile. All he said was, "Take your time, boy." He rang for a steward and ordered coffee.

"Pretty near bed-time," he said. "Let you go in a couple of minutes. Anything else you want to know from me?"

I said slowly, "Well, I guess not, sir. Not unless you can think of something I should know."

He shrugged those giant shoulders expressively. "Did I tell you about Marine Mines?" he demanded.

"Well, I know a little bit about it, from Mr. Faulkner."

"Not much, probably. Well, not much to tell. Typical fat-headed scheme of your uncle's, of course. Mine Eden Deep! Couldn't get within a thousand fathoms of the bottom—not even with his own Edenite. Tried to tell him that—but it never was any use trying to talk sense to your Uncle Stewart."

I said, as bitingly as I could, "So the mathematicians found out." When Uncle Stewart first announced his

Edenite process, the mathematicians were quick to call it impossible. They proved conclusively with facts and figures that it was ridiculous to imagine that any force-field armor could be so constructed as to make the water work against itself, turn its own pressure against it to keep the surging tides out of whatever the armor enclosed. It wasn't until Uncle Stewart managed to get the first Edenite armor in operation that the mathematicians hastily changed the subject.

Sperry grinned. "Good point, boy," he admitted. "Well, I guess I had something like that in mind. Anyway, he went ahead. Opened an office out at Seven Dome, way out of the normal mining territory, right near the Deep. Had a man in there with him—fellow named Westervelt, some such name. Don't know where he is now. Dropped out of sight when your uncle died; last I heard he was hiding out in Kelly's Kingdom, in some kind of trouble with the law. That's all there is to tell, boy. Can't tell you anything that Marine Mines ever actually accomplished, because it never accomplished anything. Just a paper corporation. With paper assets."

I said, trying to keep my temper under control, "Those assets were worth a hundred and sixty thousand dollars to somebody, paper or not."

"Who?"

"Well—I don't know who," I admitted. "Some client of Mr. Faulkner's."

"Course you don't know who," he rumbled. "Tell you, if you like. Me. I offered a hundred-sixty; you turned it down. Well, maybe you did me a favor. Wasn't worth it, of course."

I stared at him. "Why—how——"

He roared with bull-like laughter. "Why—how?" he mimicked. "Boy, you're a little wet behind the ears for Marinia! No offense, of course. Tell you why: You've got a partner in the Mines, you know."

"Well, yes, but——"

"But nothing. That partner's me. I put up money; I took twenty per cent of the stock. Was supposed to get back the rest out of profits. What profits? None, of course. But I could afford the gamble, so I took it. I lost. If I can get complete ownership of the Mines, maybe I can do something with it—I have a little influence in Marinia, you know. Might be able to get the claim time extended a couple more years; maybe something will come of it eventually. Still a gamble—and not even a gamble while I'm a minority holder. See?"

I didn't see. But I was too stubborn—too young!—to admit it. I said uncomfortably, "I—I'd better talk to Mr. Faulkner, sir. Not that I doubt anything you say, of course. But——"

"But—but," he mimicked again. He was still grinning that cold, somehow worrisome grin.

Abruptly his mood changed. He set down his coffee cup with a sharp slapping sound. "Enough," he growled. "Time for bed. Go to your room, boy; get some sleep."

He rang for the steward, who appeared in his white coat, rubbing his eyes, to open the door for me. Hallam Sperry didn't get up. As I was going out he said:

"Sleep on it, boy. Just make up your mind. Do you want to pay your uncle's debts—or pay as much as you can; take my offer for your shares and I'll forget the rest—or not? Can't make you do it; it's a gentlemen's agreement. Make up your mind."

I turned uncomfortably at the door, but Sperry had dismissed me. Without haste he stood and walked lumberingly through the far door into one of his other rooms. The steward, politely but firmly, closed the outer door in my face.

12

In Thetis Dome

At last we docked at Thetis.

The *Isle of Spain* dropped out of the darkness that had surrounded her to a flat, slightly luminous plain of blue clay. We anchored at the usual flat metal platform.

To our west was Thetis itself. Its shimmering dome bulged high into the black water. Eastward and northward were rugged black hills. South lay a Deep, and on the lip of it, a phosphorescent valley, covered with weird, tangled streamers that looked like vines, and thick growths that stood tall and erect like trees on land. They looked like vines and trees—but, I was to find, they were not. No vegetation grows so far beneath the sea's surface; all the dainty blossoms and ropy growths were animal, not plants.

I disembarked from *Isle of Spain*, checked my baggage and went directly to Faulkner's office.

W-17, S-469, Level 9—the address was well fixed in my mind. It had been on the long blue envelopes in which the checks from my uncle had come.

From the elevator I stepped into the big waiting room beneath the docks, carved out of the living rock beneath the ocean floor. It was brilliant with the cold, violet Troyon light, crowded with the passengers of the *Isle of*

Spain, customs officials and hundreds of others. It seemed incredible, in that giant chamber, that four miles of sea towered over our heads.

But it was true! I was in Marinia!

I found a passenger belt headed in the right direction, and on it I was swept swiftly down a long tunnel; I found the elevator bank I was seeking and in a matter of short minutes I was at Level 9.

I stepped out onto a rather wide street.

It was flooded with the violet Troyon light, crowded with hurrying Marinians. It was my first glimpse of the life of a city of Marinia, and, truthfully, I was less than delighted. The people seemed dingy, roughly clad; I saw a number of scarlet-clothed sea-police moving purposefully through the crowd; the voices seemed coarse and loud. And the buildings which rose a few dozen feet to support the next level above were shabbier than I had imagined.

Of course, it was not Marinia itself which was at fault. Even then, before I had seen any of the broad, beautiful residential levels, or the sweeping concourses of the administration section, I realized that this could not be typical. Level 9 was at the no-man's-land between the factory and shipping levels beneath, and the office and residential levels above; it had all the worst features of its neighbors above and below.

It seemed to me that Faulkner's office was located in an unsavory neighborhood.

Still—Faulkner was my uncle's lawyer. I stopped a red-tunic policeman and got directions to W-17, S-149.

It turned out to be a door in a dingy office building, with a long flight of steps leading up.

At the head of the steps, I emerged into a dark, low-ceilinged room, smelling of dust and stale air. Beneath the single Troyon tube, two grimy chairs and a battered desk were all the room held.

A huge man leaned back in a chair behind the desk.

His feet were propped on the desk, his gnarled hands clasped behind his shaggy head. His mouth hung open, showing yellowed teeth; the dark face was scarred and pocked.

He was snoring loudly.

I coughed. "Good afternoon," I said.

The man in the chair snorted, dropped his feet to the floor and blinked at me. "Eh?" he said thickly. Then his eyes cleared; he looked at me with more comprehension.

"What do you want?" he said sullenly.

"I'd like to see Mr. Wallace Faulkner," I told him.

The big man shook his head. "Ain't in."

"When do you expect him?"

"Dunno. Won't be back today."

I hesitated. I could do nothing until I saw this Faulkner, that was certain; and I most urgently wanted to ask him about what Hallam Sperry had told me on the *Isle of Spain*. I said:

"It's very important that I see him. Where can I find him now?"

The big man glowered at me. "Come back tomorrow," he said. "Who are you?"

"James Eden," I said.

I thought the big man's eyes widened. But all he said was, "I'll tell him."

I started to leave. I was beginning to dislike all of this: the man, the filthy, miserable office, my impression of Faulkner formed from his letters and radios.

But I had to face the affair sooner or later. I tried once more: "Sir, I *must* see Mr. Faulkner. Isn't there any possible way I can reach him today?"

The big man snarled, "I told you *no*. Come back tomorrow. First thing in the morning—you hear me?"

There was nothing to do but leave—especially since he slammed his feet down on the desk again, tilted back and seemed ready to get back to his interrupted sleep.

I let myself out the office door and started down the stairs.

Halfway down I stopped. I thought I heard the big man calling my name.

I stood there for a moment, listening. It came again, clearly, not so much as though I were being called as though the man were saying it emphatically to someone else; my name, clearly enough to recognize unmistakably, then a pause and a mumble of other words.

I went back up the stairs.

At the door I heard a final mumble: "—Eden. See you in the morning." And then the sound of a telephone handpiece being slammed down on its cradle. I waited, but there was no other sound, until a moment later I began to hear the big man's regular breathing.

He had gone to sleep—but he had phoned someone first. About me.

No, I didn't like this at all. . . .

Still, I told myself, things could be worse.

If I couldn't see Faulkner until the next morning, that meant I had almost a whole day to spend at whatever I wished. I could, for instance, look around Thetis, see all the wonders of the capital of Marinia at first hand.

My mood of depression began to lift. I stopped a scarlet-clad sea-policeman and asked him to recommend a hotel. He mentioned several, told me how to reach them, where to find a phone to make reservations.

The phone was in a drinking place, it turned out; the customers seemed mostly to be the same rough characters that were shouldering their way along the street. I didn't have to drink with them, though, after all: I found the pay telephone, located a coin and called the first hotel the policeman had suggested.

The clerk was brisk and polite. They had a room; they would hold it for me; they would expect me in an hour, as soon as I had picked up my bags.

Things were beginning to look up as I put down the phone and started back to the street. I could get my bags without trouble—the customs men would have had a chance to examine them by now if they wished—and then I had the rest of the day to myself.

As I headed for the door, a tall, lean man turned away from the bar right in front of me. I stopped, but not quite quickly enough; I jarred him slightly, and a few drops spilled from his drink.

He whirled on me. "Watch it, Mac!" he growled.

"Sorry," I said, and waited for him to step aside. But he wasn't stepping. He carefully set his drink down on the bar and moved even closer to me.

"Think you own the place?" he demanded. "Come in here looking for trouble, is that it?"

It hardly seemed reasonable—but he gave every indication of looking for a fight. I'm not afraid of a fight if I must have one; at the Academy, there had been plenty of man-to-man boxing and sometimes it was done less for exercise than to work out differences of opinion. I had carried a shiner around with me for a week after one such bout. And, though the man was inches taller than I, he weighed little more; I wasn't afraid of him.

Still—a bar-room brawl was not my idea of the best way to spend my first day in Thetis. I said, "Excuse me. I didn't mean to bump into you. Will you let me pass?"

He seemed to take that as a personal insult. "Let you pass?" he demanded. "Sure, I'll let you pass. You lubbers think you can trample all over us, don't you? Well, you're wrong!" He was actually touching me, he stood so close; I could feel his hot breath fanning me as he talked.

It looked like a fight, all right. I stepped back a bit to give myself space. . . .

Then a rumbling bass said: "What's the matter, Kelly? This kid threatening your life and limb?"

It was the sea-police. Tall and square in his scarlet tunic, he stood in the doorway. His tone was heavily humorous, but the look he gave the thin man was not humorous at all.

The thin man made a quick estimate of the situation. "Ah," he snarled, "you cops give me a pain. Why don't you mind your business?"

The policeman's eyes sparkled dangerously, but all he said was, "All right, son. If you're coming out of here, come on."

I walked past Kelly without looking at him. The policeman closed the door behind us.

"Thought you might get into trouble there," he rambled. "As soon as I sent you in to phone, I says to myself, 'Shaughnessy, a kid like that don't belong in a place like

Mother Sea-Cow's.' So I just walked over to see what might be happening."

I said, "Thanks, officer. I don't think there would have been any trouble, though."

He gave me a quizzical look. "Lubber, aren't you?" he said. "Well, never mind. Get along with you." And he stood watching while I headed for the elevator banks.

It took me only a few minutes to reclaim my baggage. Loaded with it, I studied the street and level markers, trying to find the best way to the hotel.

I suppose I should have asked someone; but I have always disliked seeming ignorant. Many's the wasted hour I have spent wandering around a strange city, stubbornly trying to find a street number by myself, when any passerby could have pointed the way in a matter of moments.

After racking my brains, I came to the conclusion that the best way to get to the hotel was to walk through a narrow connecting passage to another bank of express elevators. They would whisk me to Level 18, where the hotel was located, without stops.

Staggering under the weight of the bags, I started off. The way led through an alley of warehouses. It was the middle of the morning, but few persons were about; I suppose that, as in the cities on the earth's surface, the warehouses and markets are busiest during the pre-dawn hours, getting ready for the day's trade. Of course, under four miles of sea, the time of day made little difference; the lights were the same blue-violet Troyon tubes, though it seemed to me that these flickered more weakly than most. The warehouse fronts cast curious shadows; some of them seemed almost to be lurking human figures.

And some of them were.

I found it out to my cost. I set the bags down where another passage crossed the one I was traversing, a little doubtful as to which turn I should take. I heard footsteps behind me; nothing of any importance, it seemed, until of a sudden the steps got closer, and speeded up, as though an assailant were closing in for the kill. I turned, less in alarm than in curiosity.

I turned too late. Something hard and large came swinging through the violet-lit shadows at me. It crunched against my temple; and that was the last I saw for some time.

I awoke.

I was lying on the cold, smooth metal floor of a totally dark room.

My ankles were trussed together. A cord was about my waist; my wrists were fastened to it at my sides. The knots were so tight that the circulation was stopped, and my hands and feet were numb.

I could see nothing, feel nothing, hear nothing. My only knowledge of the room I was in came through my nose—and that was a puzzler. The room smelled stale and musty, like a damp cellar underground. Where in Thetis could such a room be?

Since I could not guess, I gave up trying. I struggled uselessly for a while; then I lay there, trying to make an estimate of the situation as coolly and dispassionately as the instructors had demanded at the Academy. I remember the lectures: "Panic is your worst enemy. No matter how bad the situation is, giving in to it will make it worse."

It had all seemed so logical and lucid, back in the warm Caribbean sunshine!

But they had never told us exactly what to do when tied up by person or persons unknown, in what seemed to be the subcellar of an undersea city. The whole thing seemed ridiculous to me. Why would anyone attack me in the first place? I had harmed no one. . . .

However, the important question at the moment was not "why," but "how"—how to get out of this. There seemed very little to do in that direction. I could scarcely move a muscle. Whoever tied me had taken lessons from a master at the art.

Still. . . . I found that I could wriggle one arm slightly. If I could find something to rub the ropes against, there was always the chance I could fray them through. Fumbling about on the floor for a sharp projection was like trying to recognize the denomination of a coin through heavy mittens; my numbed fingers had scarcely any tactile sensation left. But I kept on trying.

Fruitlessly. The floor was flat and bare.

And I could not reach any of the knots, however much I strained.

I think I gave in to desperation there for a moment. Perhaps it helped; I don't know. But I flung myself violently back against the floor. . . .

And I felt the bonds around my waist slip a little. Ever so little.

They were not coming off, of course—that was too much to hope for. But they slipped around a couple of degrees; my right hand was a little behind me now, my left hand a little in front. I wrenched at the rope again, and it slipped a fraction more.

It must have taken me half an hour to do it, but at last my left hand was within range of my belt buckle. Thanks be to the sea sprites, the Kelpies who watch over the submariners! I still wore my Academy belt, with the fouled anchors sharp on the buckle.

It was not much in the way of hope, but it was the best I had. I strained my wrist cords against that buckle, back and forth, back and forth. I kept it up until I thought my arm muscles would knot and freeze . . . and then I kept it up some more.

I began to feel as though, given time, I might get free.

But time ran out for me right then.

There was a sudden, soft clicking sound behind me. Dim light entered the room. I could see only what was directly before my eyes—smooth metal walls, glistening with a thin film of moisture; nothing more. But someone had, behind me, opened a door.

I lay perfectly still.

Sound of soft footsteps. A pause; and then the footsteps retreating.

There was another faint click as the door closed again—and darkness.

Someone had come into the room, looked at me, gone away again.

What did it mean? I could not guess. All I could imagine was that it meant someone wanted to know if I were conscious or not; I hoped I had deceived them.

I went back to my rubbing, but for only a few moments. Then the door opened again; but the footsteps were not soft.

There were several men behind me. They were talking to each other as they came in; there was no attempt at concealment, no sense of trying to disguise their voices, no seeming awareness that I was alive. That could mean only one thing:

As far as they were concerned, the time in which I would remain alive was very short.

"Sure he's awake," said one of the men belligerently. "Go on, Jack—give him a kick and see."

Jack did. His foot connected with my right shoulder blade. Somehow no bones were broken; but I have never been hit harder in my life. The impact spun me around, lying on the floor as I was; I came to rest on my other side, facing the men.

The man who had kicked me was a hulking, stubby toad of a man; I had never seen him before. One of the others was equally strange. But the third I recognized.

Kelly was his name. He had tried to pick a fight with me, back on the Ninth Level.

I said, through a haze of pain, "What's all this about? What do you——"

"Shut up," said Kelly contemptuously. "If he opens his mouth again, Jack, kick his teeth in. Come on, give me a hand."

Kelly stood back, staring expressionlessly, as Jack and the other man picked me up, head and foot. They carried me out of the room, down a short, dimly-lit corridor.

The man at my feet grunted, "Kelly, I don't like this. Suppose the sea-cops wander by?"

"Suppose the moon falls on us?" Kelly said sardonically. "You're not paid to think. Jack scouted for the cops; he said there wasn't a patrol-jeep on the whole level. Right?"

Jack growled, "Right." A man of few words, this Jack, I thought. I opened my mouth to say something, but the sudden gleam of interest in his eyes stopped me. We bumped along for a few yards, then my bearers dropped me.

"Okay," growled Kelly. "Take off, boys. I won't need you any more."

The other two left—hurriedly. Kelly came closer, and bent down beside me. He fumbled with something on the floor, out of my range of vision: I heard a heavy clanking sound.

"So long," he said, grinning at me. A sudden seepage of cold wet air came up alongside me; as Kelly raised his foot to thrust at me, I realized what he had done. He had opened a trap—beneath lay the drainage tunnels of Thetis!

As his foot came down I made a desperate lunge, and felt the cord that bound my left wrist part. But it was too late, far too late; his foot caught me in the side and thrust me over a metallic lip. I scrambled and half-caught myself; but one numbed hand was not enough.

I plunged into icy, quick-flowing water. The shock of striking it paralyzed me for a moment; I sank far down before I somehow, with one hand, began struggling upward again.

Somehow, somehow—I reached the surface. Somehow I kept myself afloat, coughing and strangling, gasping cold, dank air into my lungs, surging along through a giant metal conduit at a rate of knots, as helpless as a jellyfish in a tidal bore.

Almost I gave up; but something would not let me give up. Perhaps it was the voice of my instructors at the Academy: *Panic is the enemy.* Perhaps it was a Voice more authoritative still—but something kept me kicking and struggling, though the best I could hope for was to stay alive until I reached the vent pumps. . . .

And, in the fiercely driven pistons of the pumps, forcing the waste seepage out against a pressure of many atmospheres, the struggle would surely end.

But I kept on struggling.

And—I saw a light.

Only a dim glow, but it was a light. I saw it, far off, through a mist of salt water. I blinked and looked again, and it was closer; a dim flicker on a sort of shelf beside the surging flow.

It was a portable Troyon light. And beside it a man stood, staring at the water.

I tried to call to him, but only a splutter came out. Perhaps he heard me; perhaps it was only fortune that made him look at where I struggled. But I heard his wordless shout, and I found breath to cough a reply.

He acted like the lightning itself. Almost as soon as he had seen me I was driven to the ledge where he stood; in a moment I would have been irrecoverably gone. But just as I slid beneath him he lunged at me with what looked like a long pole.

Something sharp and painful caught my shoulder. I felt the skin break and tear as the boathook slid along my upper arm and back. The cloth of my tunic ripped, held, ripped again—

And held.

He dragged me, feebly spluttering, to his ledge and helped me up.

I slumped breathlessly against the wall. He grinned at me.

"Man," he said, "you must have wanted to go swimming *awful* bad!"

13

The Hermit of Kelly's Kingdom

"Thanks," I said, for saving my life, for risking his own—if he had slipped into that raging water, we both would have died—all I could say was "thanks."

"Sure," my rescuer said off-handedly. He studied me while I caught my breath, and I returned the compliment. He was a tall, husky Negro, dark as any Gullah, with a clear, friendly eye. He shook his head as he saw the ropes on me. "Um," he said. "Maybe you weren't swimming for fun after all." He thrust a hand far down into a trouser pocket, and drew out a clasp knife.

The pain in my fingers and toes as he cut the ropes and the blood surged back was worse than anything that had gone before. I never thought I would welcome pain! But at last I began to believe in my luck—I was alive!

"Thanks," I said inadequately again. "You saved my life; I hope I can pay back the favor."

He chuckled. "Why, I certainly hope you can't, friend," he said. "I don't exactly want to need that kind of favor. Come on, let me give you a hand." Leaning on him, I limped a few yards along the ledge to where the Troyon light lay. It was a small tube, flickering and feeble as though its luminous gas were nearly exhausted. But it was welcome light to me. By it I looked around.

There was a niche in the ledge. In the niche, barely head high and wide enough for a man to lie down, were a few tattered blankets, a rough platform of boards that appeared to serve as a bed, a few packing crates. "Welcome to my home," said the man. "My name's Park, Gideon Park. It isn't a very fancy establishment, but you're welcome to make use of it."

I said earnestly, "Mr. Park, I never saw a place I liked better."

He grinned. "I imagine so," he said. "Call me Gideon, if you don't mind; it's a name I'm partial to. That's why I made it up. My folks christened me Walter, but I guess they kind of ran out of good names after eleven of us. . . . Unless you'd like to forget the whole thing, you might satisfy an old man's curiosity. Who put the ropes on you?"

I shook my head. "I wish I knew, Mr.—Gideon, I mean. Somebody named Kelly and somebody else he called Jack. That's all I know about them. They took everything out of my pockets, so I guess that's all they wanted. Why they picked me, though—I'll never know, I guess."

Gideon frowned. "Lots of Kellys around," he said somberly. "This one wouldn't be a tall, skinny fellow with a nasty disposition, would he?"

"He certainly would. Do you know him?"

Gideon nodded. "Sorry to say I do. That's a long story, though; but you can consider yourself a lucky man. You're still alive."

I absorbed that thoughtfully. My fingers and toes were beginning to feel as though they might some day be of use to me again. I tried standing up; I was wobbly as a jellyfish in a riptide, but I made it. I flexed my leg muscles and my fingers. I would ache for quite a while, I knew, but nothing appeared to be broken.

I was, of course, sopping wet. Gideon and I realized it at the same moment. He said, "Slip out of those things, friend, and I'll make a little fire. As long as you aren't going to drown for a while yet, we might as well keep you from getting pneumonia." He broke a few loose boards over his knee, teepeed them over an ancient, crumpled newssheet and lit the structure. It burned smokily in the damp air; but in a moment the fire itself drove the dampness out of its fuel and the flames shot high. Gideon hung my clothes near the fire, and I moved close to its warmth. He began rattling odds and ends of gear. "Long as I've got a fire, we might as well have a cup of tea. It'll do us both good." He put water on to boil and sat back on his haunches comfortably enough. He must have noticed the curiosity in my eyes, because he chuckled.

"Wondering what you've got yourself into, aren't you?" he asked. "I suppose the old homestead looks pretty peculiar to someone like you."

I said, "Well, I admit I was a little curious."

Gideon nodded. "It's a living," he said easily. "All manner of things come down the drains. Thetis is pretty far underwater, you know. The pressure is a mite terrific; water seeps in through the rock itself. So they have to keep pumping; and as long as they're pumping the water out anyhow, they use the drains for disposing of all sorts of objects. Some are pretty worthless. Others are just curiosities—like, for instance, yourself." He grinned at me. "But every once in a while something comes by that I can sell. So I fish it out and lay it aside, and when I've got enough to make the trip worth while I head on up to the living levels, and try my hand at peddling. I usually get enough to stock in food and tea and such other necessities. . . . And then I come back home to Kelly's Kingdom."

"Kelly's Kingdom?" I repeated. "Any relation to the Kelly we were talking about?"

Gideon shrugged. "They called the sub-levels Kelly's Kingdom thirty years ago," he said. "The Kelly you're acquainted with probably wasn't born then. I have an idea he named himself after the place instead of vice-versa." He looked at me pointedly. "Names, after all, are a person's own business. For instance, I picked my own. And, again, you no doubt have a name, but since you don't choose to mention it, no gentlemen would seek to embarrass you by——"

"Oh, I'm sorry, Gideon," I interrupted apologetically. "James Eden is my name."

The grin was gone from his face as though it had never been.

"What?" he demanded.

I blinked at him. "James Eden," I repeated. "I—I'm Stewart Eden's nephew . . . perhaps you know of him."

He stood up and stared down at me, his face a mask. "James Eden," he said, and that was all he said for a long moment.

He reached down with a long arm, grasped my hand, yanked me to my feet. I came up almost belligerently, almost expecting a fight; his expression was unreadable.

But his handclasp on mine was powerful and warm. "Jim," he said, "I worked for Stewart for nine years. I'd be working for him now if he were alive—and if he'd have me. Your uncle Stewart saved my life twice, so I reckon you're even with me for this last one, and I owe you one to boot. . . ."

They were the first friendly words I had heard spoken since I left Bob Eskow in New York, so long before. I almost disgraced myself, the Academy that had cast me out, my Uncle Stewart and the whole sub-sea life. I almost blubbered.

But then the water was boiling and Gideon made us tea. While we were sipping the first steam-hot gulps he told me what he could about my uncle Stewart. Gideon himself had been a bottom-walker—one of those rugged individualists who puts on deep-sea armor and wades through the sludge and ooze under steep miles of pressure. He'd mined for Uncle Stewart in the Mountains of Darkness, drilled test borings for him in the oil prospects, searched side by side with him for pearl shell and precious pearls themselves in the Kadang beds. When Uncle Stewart sold out his other holdings to concentrate on Marine Mines Ltd., Gideon had refused other jobs; he'd come down to Kelly's Kingdom, to swamp the sewers, to be ready to go back to Uncle Stewart the minute Stewart needed him.

But Gideon knew little of Marine Mines; I asked him eagerly, but he told me no more than Hallam Sperry already had said.

Since Uncle Stewart's death, Gideon had been trying to make plans—and failing; everything he wanted to do was founded on going back to work for my uncle. On the spot I offered him a job—duties unspecified, salary whatever he thought I should pay him, as long as my money held out. On the spot, he took it—and laughed at the idea of being paid a salary. "You're talking just like your uncle," he grumbled. "Offered to work for him for nothing; he wouldn't let me. You keep us both eating and out of trouble with the law for vagrancy, and that's all the salary I want till we get things straightened out."

I was exhausted; and I could no longer stay awake. Gideon threw blankets together on the platform for me, and I fell asleep.

But when I slept, it was in the full knowledge that at last I had met a friend and comrade. Almost I blessed Kelly for tossing me in the drain!

When we woke, Gideon made us more tea and rustled up food. My clothes were dry but far from neat; Kelly's comrades had looted my pockets, but missed the currency in the compartment behind my Academy belt-buckle. So Gideon and I went shopping.

By the time we were dressed fit for travel, it was night again. The Troyon lights of the sub-sea cities mark neither day nor night; but human beings need sleep, and so the cities keep to the time zones of the world above. On the off chance that I might catch Faulkner in, I called the lawyer's office; but there was no answer. Gideon and I spent the evening seeing the sights of Thetis. A pleasurable, relaxing experience it was. I felt at peace with the world when finally we turned in—not in Gideon's submarine cave of the drain-pipes, but in a modest, clean, comfortable lodging house he recommended.

It was the last time I felt at peace with the world for some time. . . .

The next morning I went direct to Faulkner's office.

I took the inevitable elevator to Level Nine. Once more I climbed the long, dark stair; once more I entered the room.

The plug-ugly behind the desk was awake this time; he sat reading a newssheet, his feet as before plumped on the desk.

When he saw me his eyes widened incredulously and his jaw dropped. He peered silently at me, unbelievingly; then he recovered himself. "You," he grumbled. But his expression was as strained as that of a man who has seen a ghost.

"Yes, me," I said. "Is Mr. Faulkner in now?"

He glowered at me. His Neanderthal brain was obviously trying to reach a difficult decision. He grunted, and said: "I'll go see."

He lifted his gross body with astonishing vigor, rolled across the room and vanished through a door with Faulkner's name on it. I stood waiting for long minutes; then he came back and snarled, "Go on in."

The room I entered was a little larger than the Neanderthal's, but dark and low-ceilinged. The walls were lined with rows of ancient books, the leather of their bindings cracking and peeling; the air was musty, dusty, redolent of dry rot.

Beneath the one dim Troyon tube, Faulkner sat staring coldly at me. He was a nondescript human—medium tall, medium thin, medium sallow and wrinkled, medium elderly. His black suit was rather worn for a successful attorney's; it was also not very clean. His eyes were hard behind thick-lensed eyeglasses.

I said, "Mr. Faulkner?"

He sat very erect, palms pressed against his desk. "I am," he said crisply. "And you claim to be James Eden."

I looked at him curiously. "I *am* James Eden," I corrected. "You radioed me several times about my uncle's estate, Mr. Faulkner. I told you I was coming here to claim it. Did you get my radio?"

His stare remained cold. "Hum," he said. And then,

obliquely, "Why didn't you keep your appointment yesterday?"

I said, with some irritation, "Because I was mugged and robbed, Mr. Faulkner. I'm sorry if it inconvenienced you."

"Hum," he said. His hawklike face expressed neither surprise nor sympathy. "What do you want?"

"Why—well, as I wrote you, I want to take possession of my uncle's estate."

He said disagreeably, "Do you indeed! And just who might your uncle be?"

I stared at him, hardly believing I was hearing right. "My uncle Stewart Eden," I said in some confusion. "You know him, Mr. Faulkner!"

"I *knew* him. Stewart Eden is dead, young man." I started to say something, but he clipped on, one hand raised to restrain me: "Furthermore, I should like to see some identification from you."

I said hotly: "I told you, Mr. Faulkner—I was robbed! All my identification is gone."

He looked skeptical. He said: "Hum!"

"But that's what really happened," I insisted. "I——"

The hand was raised again. "Enough, young man!" he said sharply. "There is no point in continuing with this. As an attorney, permit me to acquaint you with the law. Imposture for the purpose of criminal gain—posing as the heir to an estate, for instance—is a serious offense. My advice to you is to give it up."

I was stunned. "What?" I demanded.

"You understood me, I believe. You are not James Eden. I do not know who you are, but it is certain that him you are not."

I cried, "Listen, Mr. Faulkner, you're making a mistake! I *am* James Eden."

He shouted, "And I say you are not! I have met James Eden—right here, in this office! You look no more like him than you do like me!"

I gaped at him. "Wh-what?"

"Impostor!" he raged. "Get out of my office! Now—

and get down on your knees and thank me for not turning you over to the police!"

I burst out, "See here, Mr. Faulkner, this is ridiculous. Of course I'm James Eden—I can prove it!"

He said explosively, "Do so!"

I hesitated. "Well," I admitted, "it will take a little time. I'll have to send back to the States for my papers. . . ."

"Liar!" he cried. "You dare say that, when I have in my desk here the identification book of the real James Eden, with his picture, fingerprints and all the rest!"

I gaped. "You—you what?" I asked feebly.

He thrust a hand into a drawer. "See for yourself," he said harshly, tossing a familiar little red book before me. I picked it up apprehensively. . . .

Familiar?

I had carried it for many years. It was not an imitation of my book—it *was* my book, to the last crease and ink spot and blurred line.

But the picture in it was not of me. The man was a total stranger; the description fit him, not me; the signature was not my own.

Faulkner snatched the book away from me. "Bishop!" he called. The Neanderthaler rolled in from the other room, and stood regarding me eagerly. To me, Faulkner said coldly: "Get out!"

What else could I do?

Gideon explained it—perhaps. "Your friend Mr. Faulkner must have had you mugged," he speculated. "I would imagine, Jim, that he wants you out of the way pretty badly, to go as far as murder."

"But the identification book, Gideon!" I said.

He shook his head. "Jim," he said patiently, "there are men in Thetis who could forge any document the world has ever seen. It isn't hard for someone who knows how. The question isn't 'how'; the question is 'why.' I don't like to leap at conclusions, but the one that suggests itself most quickly is: Marine Mines Limited are worth more than they seem to be."

I shook my head bewilderedly. "But they can't be," I said. "It's all below the depth limit, the whole prospect—even if Uncle Stewart had found something there, there's no way of getting it out."

Gideon shrugged. "Have you a better idea?"

I had to confess I didn't. We sat wordless for a moment. Then I said: "Well, what shall I do? Go back and get thrown out of Faulkner's office again?"

Gideon shook his head, and a gleam of anticipation came into his eye. "Not this time, Jim. First you establish your identity—go to the consul here in Thetis, get a duplicate of your papers. *Then* we go back to see Faulkner. You and me both. And I would like to see us get thrown out; it would be quite a spectacle, Jim."

I did as Gideon suggested.

The office of the immigration inspector was up with the other government buildings, on Level Twenty-one.

I stated my case to an assistant at the passport window. He nodded non-committally, excused himself, then returned to take me to the office of the Inspector himself.

He was a plump, bald, brisk-mannered little man named Chapman. He shook my hand pleasantly, listened to my story and nodded understandingly.

"That sort of thing happens," he said. "Pity, but it does. We can help you, young man." He rang a bell; his secretary showed me the way to the laboratory.

I was stripped, measured, weighed, fingerprinted, retina-printed, photographed with natural light, fluorescence and X-rays. I was examined, poked and probed; my teeth were counted and charted; the pores on the soles of my feet were located and graphed. The process took well over an hour.

When it was finished, a white-smocked lab attendant brought me back to the Inspector.

Inspector Chapman handed me a passport, which bore in scarlet letters the legend TEMPORARY. "Carry this for the next two weeks," he instructed. "By then we will have word from the United States; if your statistics match the information our laboratory sends them, we'll issue you a new permanent passport. This one, I'm sorry to say, will not do you much good except to permit you to travel about Thetis. You can't leave without a permanent passport."

"And you'll have that in two weeks?" I asked. "Thank you very much, sir."

He escorted me to the door. "Not at all," he said. "It's part of our job to help out when someone loses an important document." He looked at me levelly. "Always assuming," he added, "that the document is really theirs to begin with."

The door closed on his last words.

14

The Outcasts of Marinia

So we had to wait—wait until the mixup on my papers could be straightened out, wait until we could have a showdown with Faulkner, wait until I could learn the answers to many questions.

We had time to kill, Gideon and I. We spent it looking around the dome-city of Thetis. Gideon knew it well, from the high administrative levels to the sub-cellars below the very sea floor. And he showed me everything there was.

He took me to the great submarine quays, not the liner terminals where I had docked in the *Isle of Spain*, but the freight ports where the commerce of the sub-sea world was carried on. Through the view ports in the side of the dome we could see, floodlighted, a busy hustle of ungainly freighters and tiny, porpoiselike sea cars, nuzzling down to the discharge ports, slipping up and away to the other cities of Marinia. We watched a lumbering tanker as it made five unsuccessful passes at the port—"Tough job for them," Gideon chuckled; "they're lighter than the water, and it's hard to swim them in just right." I nodded and stared, wide-eyed. Lighter than the water! Yet it was obvious—their cargoes of petroleum and its products needed more than the mere weight of the cargo hulk to equal an identical volume of sea water. Through the view ports one was hardly aware of the water outside: it looked like some curious scene of interplanetary space, with the sub-sea ships taking the parts of rockets. The muck in suspension in the water around Thetis made it cloudy, but it was more like a land fog than an undersea view. I could even see, dimly, the face of the tanker-pilot as he raged at his engineer through the intercom as they made their fruitless passes—and then his smile of triumph as the grapples locked, and they were moored. He was not alone in the bridgehouse; beside him were men in the uniform of the Maritime Service—

And one of them was no stranger! "Bob!" I gasped. "Bob Eskow!"

Gideon looked at me curiously. "An acquaintance of yours?" he asked.

"Just the best friend I have in the world, that's all! Gideon, this is wonderful luck! How can we get to that tanker?"

He scratched his head doubtfully. "I don't know if it's a good idea," he objected mildly. "You know, Jim, we still haven't figured out what Kelly was up to when he mugged you. And that's Kelly's Kingdom down there, where the freighters discharge——"

My expression must have convinced him. He grinned and surrendered. "All right. Come on," he said.

We took a fast elevator down, but it seemed to take terribly long. At the discharge level we came out onto a badly lighted, poorly kept section of Thetis, much like the one I had come in at, but even worse in appearance if possible. There were the same long rows of warehouses, the same jostling, bustling crowds of dock workers. I stayed close by Gideon's side as he struck out confidently.

But there was no trouble—not the sort of trouble I might have feared, at any rate. There was no sign of Kelly; no one even looked at us, much less tried to repeat Kelly's attack. What actually happened was much, much worse.

We reached the tanker—*S.S. Warren F. Howard* was its name—and rode the little pneumatic lift to the entrance port. I stopped a crewman and asked directions to the bridge; with Gideon in tow, I raced along the narrow passageways and climbed through a hatchway to the bridgehouse.

Bob wasn't there.

The pilot was talking casually to a deck officer; they turned to look at me with some irritation. I asked excitedly, "Is Bob Eskow here? I saw him from the dome——"

The pilot said something in a whisper. The deck man nodded thoughtfully. He said: "Who wants him?"

"My name," I told him, "is——"

Gideon's elbow caught me sharply in the ribs. He interrupted smoothly, "Just a couple of old friends of his, sir. Can you tell us where we can find him?"

The deck officer glowered. "How did you get aboard?" he demanded.

"Just walked, sir," Gideon said with a wide-eyed look of innocence. "Was that wrong?"

The deck officer gave him a long look. Then, to me, he said: "You'll have to go ashore. Eskow's in his quarters and can't be disturbed."

"But I just saw him!" I cried.

"You heard me." The deck officer touched a bell, and a seaman popped through the hatch. "Show these men ashore," the officer ordered.

Unwillingly I went. Back on the other side of the entrance port, I asked the seaman: "Can you take a message to Mr. Eskow for me?"

The seaman looked dubious, until he caught sight of my outstretched hand and the folded bill it contained. "Sure," he said cheerfully. "What do you want me to tell him?"

I wrote a hasty note, signed it "Jim," and handed it to the seaman, who disappeared into the entrance port with it. Gideon murmured:

"Don't know if that was rightly smart, Jim. Know what ship this is?"

I shook my head. Gideon whispered: "Hallam Sperry's tanker flagship. And that first officer is one of his personal pets, Jim; that's why I didn't want you telling him who you were."

I said uncertainly, "But surely he wouldn't have kept me from seeing an old friend!"

"Are you so very sure of that?" Gideon asked quietly. But I had no chance to answer, for the seaman was back. His face was extremely cold. He said:

"Mr. Eskow says he never heard of you." And he disappeared again before I could collect my wits to answer.

Back in our hotel, I stared out the window at the bustling crowds of Marinians. Even Bob Eskow seemed to have turned against me! Except for Gideon, there seemed no one I could trust in all the world.

I never felt so lonesome in my life as at that moment.

I sat there, fruitlessly worrying, until Gideon came in. He had sent me on ahead while he ran some mysterious errand of his own, down in Kelly's Kingdom; when he came into the room his face was grave. He said at once:

"Jim, something's up. There's talk down at the 'charge levels. Sperry's got something."

"What has he got?"

Gideon looked worried. "That's just it, I don't know. Ever hear of a man named Catroni?"

"No."

Gideon's face was in harsh lines. "Fortunate for you," he said. "Catroni. Kicked out of the States, kicked out of every country in Europe, on Hallam Sperry's payroll here in Marinia. Payroll for what? Nobody knows—officially. But the man started out as a common hoodlum. Draw your own conclusions."

"Sounds like someone you couldn't trust very far," I said.

Gideon nodded soberly. "That is the trouble, Jim. Somebody trusted him a little too far. He was with your uncle when the sea-car was lost. And they say—" He hesitated, looking at me almost beseechingly. "They say—don't draw too much hope from this, Jim, but they say that Catroni was seen going into Sperry's quarters yesterday."

I leaped up. "Gideon! That means—"

He said fretfully, "I know what it means. *If* it's true that Catroni is here—and *if* he really was with Stewart Eden—

then *maybe* there's a chance. A chance of heaven knows what, Jim—for if Catroni came back secretly, there must be dirty work somewhere that he is covering up. But still—"

"Gideon," I said tensely, "let's go see Hallam Sperry!"

He stared. "You are out of your mind!"

"No, Gideon. I can see him. I have his invitation, after all—on the *Isle of Spain* he made me an offer. I can tell him I want to discuss it; and perhaps I can find something out." Gideon was shaking his head somberly, but I rushed on. "Don't you see, Gideon, I have to try it. Sperry won't dare do anything openly—he has too much at stake. And besides—well, I'll lay it on the line, Gideon: Suppose you're wrong? Suppose Sperry isn't quite as bad as you've painted him?"

He stopped me, mercifully, then. There was fierce pride and hurt in his eyes. He said carefully: "All right, Jim. I can't blame you for wanting to see for yourself." He slumped wearily into a chair, not looking at me. "I only hope," he said, "that what you see doesn't hurt you."

"SIT, SIT," Hallam Sperry rumbled impatiently.

I sat down. I started to say, "Mr. Sperry, I—"

He interrupted before I got started. "My son is here," he said suddenly. "Brand. You remember Brand, eh? Told me a great deal about you. Maybe I should say about James Eden. Eh?"

The question seemed half-humorous, but his cold eyes were not humorous at all. "What do you mean?" I asked.

He shrugged ponderously. "What do you want?" he asked.

He had me somewhat confused. I said, "Well, back on the *Isle of Spain* you made a proposition, Mr. Sperry."

I stopped. He was shaking his huge head. "Forget that," he said. "I'm an old man. I bear no grudge for you trying to take me in, but it didn't work." He stared at me out of his sea-cold eyes. "You're no more James Eden than I am," he said. "You know it, I know it, what's the use of trying to pull the wool over an old man's eyes?"

I said, trying to control my temper, "Mr. Sperry, I *am*

James Eden! I was knocked out and robbed—my papers
were stolen—but I'm getting new ones from 'Frisco."

He laughed shortly. "That's it, boy," he applauded.
"Stick to it!"

"Please, Mr. Sperry! Look, you say your son is here—
ask him to identify me."

Hallam Sperry looked at me for a long, opaque moment. Then he rose ponderously and turned his back
while he 'poured himself some sort of drink. Without
turning he said: 'Brand?"

A voice came promptly from a speaker-diaphragm over
Hallam Sperry's desk. "Yes, sir?"

Hallam Sperry said: "Brand, have you been watching us
on the scanner?"

"Yes, father," came the metallic voice strongly. "He's
an impostor, sir. I never saw him before."

"Thank you, Brand," the old man said mildly. He
clicked a switch on his desk and sat down, sipping his
drink. He looked at me with his cold, inquiring eyes.
"Eh?" He asked. "Still want to argue?"

All at once the world looked tremendously black. I could
only sit there, staring at him. Had everyone gone insane?
How could Brand Sperry deny that I was James Eden?

And then I remembered the words that had helped me
once before, the words the instructors had dinned, dinned,
dinned into me at the Academy, the most urgent lesson
the Academy's four hard years could teach:

Panic is the enemy.

Start with one fact: I knew I was sane.

Look at all the other facts in the light of that one: *If* I
am sane, then I really am James Eden; *if* I am James
Eden, then these people, all of them, the Sperrys and their
helpers, are trying to get me out of the way.

And if they are trying to get me out of the way—then
certainly there is something they must fear! Something
that I can do—something that they want to prevent—
something that I must find out about and accomplish!

It takes a long time to tell what passed through my
mind in that one frozen moment; but it took no time at all
for me to decide what to do next.

Where's Catroni?"

Mr. Sperry. If Catroni survived, maybe my uncle did too.

Hallam Sperry unfroze slowly, like a giant berg of the

The bottle of sea-green liqueur splintered against the

to Hallam Sperry. "Catroni was with my uncle Stewart,

that. I want to talk to him." I stood up and moved closer

floor. Hallam Sperry sat icily calm, ignoring the bottle he

had knocked over. He said in a colorless voice, "Would

you mind repeating that?"

I said, "Where's Catroni? He's here somewhere; I know

I said boldly, "Where's Catroni?"

Crash.

Southern Ocean; he said quietly, "Catroni is dead."

"No, sir," I said obstinately. "He's alive. I know that."

"You know wrong, young man. Catroni is dead." There

was a flicker of something I could not recognize in those

sea-cold eyes. Triumph, perhaps, or hidden laughter. He

said, "Perhaps you don't believe me."

"I do not," I said sharply.

"Of course not," he nodded. "We never believe news we

don't like. Well, young man, let me convince you." He

clicked the switch again. "Brooks," he said without raising

his voice, "this young gentleman would like to know if

Catroni is dead or alive. Will you show him?"

"Yes, sir," said a man's voice over the speaker. There

was a pause; then the door opened, and a short, squat

wrestler-type stood there, blinking at us. He was dressed in

outlandishly unsuitable clothing, considering his hulking

build and anthropoid brow; he wore the livery of an

old-fashioned butler. "Sir?" he asked.

"This one, Brooks," rumbled Hallam Sperry. "Take

him and convince him that Catroni is dead. Let him see

the—evidence."

I should have been suspicious. Well, I *was* suspicious—

but not sure. And even if I had been sure, if I had known

as certainly as I knew the Sub-sea Oath, word by word

and line by line, that Hallam plotted treachery—what

could I have done?

Nothing. Nothing more than I did. I followed the brute

in butler's garb down a tapestry-hung corridor, through an inconspicuous door, into a tiny, white-walled room.

There was a dead man in the room—a short, dark-complected man who lay on a narrow table, a curious metallic affair on his head, wires leading from it to a clicking, purring machine that loomed along the sides of the room.

I recognized the machine; I had seen it once, or one like it—at the Academy. They called it a brainpump; an electronic apparatus that could seize the thoughts from a man's mind, tear secrets from a living brain. It was a giant, ugly machine, and in my mind's eye I could see the placard that had been on the one in the Academy's museum:

THE USE OF THIS MACHINE HAS BEEN OUT-LAWED BY INTERNATIONAL COVENANT. EVEN IN SMALL DOSES, EXPOSURE TO IT PRODUCES BRAIN DAMAGE. PROLONGED EXPOSURE IN-VARIABLY CAUSES DEATH.

The apelike "butler" said thickly, "You wanted to see Catroni? That's him. Dead all right, ain't he?"

I said sharply, "You've killed him! He wasn't drowned with my uncle—perhaps my uncle wasn't drowned at all! I'm going to report this to—"

The ape reached out a casual arm and cuffed me. There was tremendous power on those sloping shoulders and long arms; I spun half dazed, across the room. I heard his voice dimly as he contemptuously said, "Shut up." He walked out and closed the door behind him.

Time passed. I tried the door, knowing what the result would be. Locked. I was trapped. I sat there, in the room with that dead man and the clicking, purring machine, contemplating the catastrophe of my plans.

The door opened. It was the butler; with him, hands bound, eyes blazing anger, was a tall black man. Gideon!

"You got company," the "butler" chortled. "I'll leave you two boys together; you got lots to talk about."

He shoved Gideon staggering into the room.

The door locked upon us.

15

At the Bottom of the Deeps

Time passed. Gideon and I talked briefly; then there was nothing more to talk about. He had been waiting for me outside Sperry's quarters; he had been attacked from behind and dragged in. We were prisoners.

Gideon had been right.

Gideon roamed restlessly around the room, peering and poking and searching; I sat quietly, trying to work things out in my mind. We were truly in a bad spot. Whatever doubts I had had about Hallam Sperry were now resolved; he was an outlaw, the mayor of Marinia, certainly, but he was an outlaw nonetheless. As prisoners in his home, we were helpless. And we couldn't hope for outside aid, for who was there to help us? Bob Eskow had denied that he knew me—if indeed he ever got my message. The police—well, to help us they would have to know that we were in difficulties, and that they were not likely to know. My own credentials were confused; if I failed to turn up for the replacements the Immigration authorities would doubtless forget the whole thing. And Gideon was something of an outlaw himself, an indigent from Kelly's Kingdom, with no family and no close friends to worry about his absence.

No, there was no hope of help from outside.

And little we could do from within. I sat.

Then Gideon said: "Jim! Come over here."

I looked at him. He was standing by the clicking, humming machine, holding something in his hand—a reel of metallic thread. "Jim," he said excitedly, "this was on the intake reel. It must be what was extracted from Catroni there."

I walked over to him, skirting the body on the table. It seemed a low, ghoulish business to me, picking at the privacy of a dead man's brain; I said, "What about it?"

Gideon put the reel on the machine. "I don't know," he said. "I don't know what's in it; but it must have been something important, for Hallam Sperry to kill Catroni to get it. These machines are not very well thought of, Jim; it is not likely that Sperry advertises the fact he owns one. Let's find out what he did with it."

He threaded the metal through a scanning head and turned a switch; it began slowly to revolve and slide through the magnetic scanner. He picked up a couple of headsets, smaller than that on the dead man but much like it in design. He put one on his own close-cropped head, handed the other to me.

I put it on—and at once I was hundred of miles away. I was in another man's mind. I was seeing what he saw, feeling what he felt; I was watching a scene that had been played months before, far away.

They were in the seacar—Catroni and my uncle Stewart, and a man named Westervelt—the one Sperry had mentioned as having "dropped out of sight." Cynical humor!

I could hear them talking to each other as though I were there; I could see them walking about, working the ship, manipulating all the dials and levers and gears that sent the seacar on its way down, and farther down.

For this was my uncle's own seacar, armored with his own new Edenite shell, planned to stand a pressure far greater than any that had gone before.

The seacar was six miles down now—six miles, and going farther. New records were being set at every fathom; and the milky, glowing armor of Edenite was holding out the titanic pressures of the farthest deeps without a strain.

My uncle Stewart clapped Catroni on the back. "It's working," he chuckled, in his soft, whispering voice. Catroni nodded impatiently, eyes fixed on the depth gauges before him. There was a whisper in the helmet I wore of Catroni's own thoughts then—a dark, dangerous whisper that was not in words. I shuddered, listening and watching; and I felt I knew what was to come.

The car went deeper and deeper, while the engineer Westervelt kept the screws turning and Catroni matched the rising levels of liquid in his buoyancy tanks. Stewart Eden, conning the little ship, was a triumphant bronze-bearded figure of a man like some ancient Norse mariner battling against the devil-gods of the fierce Atlantic.

The view was cloudy at times, as though Catroni's attention had been on some inward thoughts, screened out by the selective electronic filters of the brainpump, rather than on the scene he was participating in. But I could see enough to know what was happening. I could see the little seacar go careening down until, nearly eight miles below the swells of the Pacific's surface, the glimmering hull touched murky bottom and stopped.

There was a cloudy lapse of time, as though Catroni was guarding his thoughts even from himself. But I caught glimpses. Glimpses of my uncle, Westervelt and Catroni himself by turns putting on gleaming Edenite armor, testing the locks, stepping out onto the sea floor. There was little enough to see, in truth. The brilliant floodlights of the seacar, visible fifty miles off on the surface, were damped and blackened within yards in the opaque, crushing waters at the bottom of the deep. And the bottom itself was featureless mud.

Catroni and my uncle came inside together, Westervelt standing at the lock pumps to admit them. Then Westervelt and my uncle disappeared into the engine room aft.

• • •

And Catroni did the job he had been paid to do.

While they were gone, Catroni murdered the seacar.

He destroyed the life of the ship as ruthlessly as ever, in the old days, he had blotted out the life of another gangster with his hammering machine gun.

While Westervelt and my uncle were aft, Catroni shorted out and discharged three whole tiers of the cold-coil cells that held the lifeblood of the ship's power. He flooded all the ballast tanks, and then smashed the marvelous pumps that Stewart Eden had designed to clear them, against any pressure. He systematically destroyed the sonic beam communication equipment.

Then he waited for my uncle and Westervelt to come forward again. When they did, he slipped aft, trusting that they would not look at the dials or gauges, knowing that no hint of his work was otherwise visible—for the covers had been replaced on the smashed pumps, and the cold-coil cells looked as they always had.

Aft, at the lock, Catroni disabled the suits of Edenite armor that Westervelt and my uncle had worn. His own he left intact. . . .

And the first warning the other two had of what he had done was when they heard the lock opening to the outer depths as he fled.

In his Edenite armor, Catroni lingered near the seacar for half an hour. He knew, surely, that neither Westervelt nor my uncle would give up easily; he waited to see what move they would make.

He saw. Ponderously, slowly, the lock door behind him closed again. In Catroni's mind, as we saw it in the reel from the brainpump, was cold wonder and a hint of almost contemptuous admiration.

Closing the lock door in itself was an astonishing feat. Somehow the two he had left to die had stripped the cold-coil cells of the last dregs of their power, in order to run the motors that closed the door. It would be hopeless to try to pump the water out of the lock; all they could hope to do would be to open the inner door and let the trapped water spill into the little seacar. It would make life just that much more miserable; and the energy they used would steal from them days and weeks of life, for once the cells were drained entirely the cold would kill them—if the failure of the charge on the Edenite armor of the seacar did not admit the crushing pressure of the sea to kill them first.

But they tried it.

And they had managed to repair one of the suits of armor.

We felt, in Catroni's mind, consternation and fear. He watched the lock door open again, watched a slow-moving figure in glimmering armor step wearily out; and we could feel his silent battle with himself as he hesitated and wondered if he should attack the man who dared live on, there on the bottom of the deep.

But—the ocean did Catroni's work for him.

The armor had been wrecked indeed. Jury-rigged, patched and faltering, the armor was not equipped to stand against the pressures that bore against it.

Catroni, hidden outside the last rays of the weakly glimmering seacar's floodlights, saw the armored figure move a little away from the car, across the blue mud. He saw the man trying to start the tiny propeller that would lift him to safety, saw the gleaming arm raise confidently—

Then one whole side of the armor went black!

The Eden effect, that miraculous activation of the molecules of metal that forces pressure to fight itself, lasts only so long as the milky glow of power lasts in the film that coats it. When it dims and dies—the armor becomes mere metal, and utterly unable to resist the crushing immensities that drove down upon them where they stood.

The dark side of the man's armor flattened like creased tin in a giant hydraulic press. The other side swelled, and suddenly went dark. A thin bubble formed and went spinning upward out of sight.

And some vagrant current drifted the body away.

Catroni waited a moment more, against the faint chance that the other man in the seacar, whoever he might be, would try the fatal adventure too. Then, satisfied, Catroni switched the propeller of his own intact armor on, and the power in his shoulder pack carried him up, seven miles and more, to where a chartered amphibian diving-vessel waited in rendezvous. . . .

We might have seen more. But we had seen enough; and we were interrupted.

There was an alien roaring, and I felt someone clutch at me. The helmet was jerked from my head, and the distant visions went out like a turned-off lamp.

The apelike butler was grinning at me, Hallam Sperry standing just behind.

"Busybodies you are, gentlemen," rumbled Hallam Sperry with sinister good humor. "Poking and prying. Well, we left you here and I don't suppose I have a right to complain."

I tried to get at him, but the giant strength of the squat "butler's" arms held me easily. "Sperry," I yelled, "you hired that gangster to kill my uncle!"

Sperry shrugged. "Why, perhaps I did," he agreed. "We play for high stakes here, young man. One uses whatever methods are necessary. The means don't matter—as long as you win!"

I felt Gideon, behind him, tensing to make a jump at Sperry; but the butler saw it too. He dropped me and jumped back, pulling a gun from his pocket. "Hold it," he warned thickly.

Hallam Sperry chuckled. "Sit down, gentlemen," he ordered. "Brooks here will be more comfortable, and so will you."

Brooks. I looked at the squat man again, a name ringing in my mind. "Oh," I saw slowly. "Stupid of me. I remember you now. You were one of the men who jumped me and threw me in the drainage tube."

Sperry nodded enthusiastically. "You are very perceptive," he said. "Very correct; he was. But that's over and done with, so let's forget it. Question is, what do we do with you now?"

"The same as you did with my uncle, I suppose," I said bitterly. "You'd kill me without a qualm."

"Oh, certainly. Perhaps I'll have to. But I wish——" Sperry looked at me speculatively— "I wish I had a little more information. That fool Catroni, as you perhaps saw for yourself, was a little hasty. His orders were to wait until Stewart Eden logged the results of his expedition before scuttling them. He was worried, perhaps, that the surface vessel wouldn't wait for him; at any rate he left a little prematurely. As a result, I don't know the one thing that I want to know most of all: Is there or is there not uranium at the bottom of the Deep?"

The butler, Brooks, said eagerly, "Want to brainpump them, Mr. Sperry?"

Sperry shook his head. "Patience, Brooks," he rumbled. "Young man, you know what the brainpump can do. I had to use it on Catroni because I couldn't believe he was as stupid as it seemed; I thought, unjustly as it turned out, that he was holding out on me. He died as a result of my suspicion. Not comfortably; the brainpump is not comfortable for its subjects." He looked at me narrowly, then went on in a meditative tone. "I don't really suppose," he continued, "that you know any more about your uncle's affairs than I do. But I need not chance being wrong. I could quite easily put you under the brainpump and find out, once and for all. Of course, after I do that, you know, you will be dead."

I said tightly, "You can't bluff me, Sperry!"

"Oh, I never bluff. I am just considering the possibilities. And I won't try to hide from you the fact that I don't want you dead just now. You still do own that stock. I want it. With you dead, the stock would go to your heirs, whoever they might be. If they turned up, I'd have them to reckon with; if they couldn't be found, the surrogate's court would step in to protect their interests for some future date. You understand that I have a great deal of influence here in Marinia; such an event would not be a catastrophe. But it would be—inconvenient."

I said, "What do you want?"

He said sharply, "The stock. Sign it over to me."

"And then what?" I demanded. "Then you kill us?"

Sperry spread his hands. He said gently, "What can I say?" He stepped closer, his eyes burning into mine. He said, in a tone that was still mild and gentle: "I can tell you this much: There are worse things than merely being killed, young man." We locked gazes for a long moment. Then he blinked, and was a gentle old man again. He said:

"I tell you everything in my mind, you see. Open and above-board; it always pays. I want you to understand my position very clearly, Mr. Eden. I have some of the stock in Marine Mines; I want it all. I have your uncle's first experimental seacar, with the same sort of armor on it as the one that Catroni—ah—neutralized for me. I imagine it will work just as well. If there is uranium there, I mean to have it. The world will pay through the nose for it, Mr. Eden. Perhaps they will pay in money; perhaps in other things. For the world is short of uranium; and the man who owns enough of it can own the world."

There was a sudden animal flare in his eyes; for a moment I caught a glimpse of the real Hallam Sperry, the wolfman who would destroy anything for ultimate power; then it died away.

Hallam Sperry sighed heavily and turned away. "Take care of these two, Brooks," he said over his shoulder. "I'll want to talk to them again in a little while."

He was gone, the door closing behind him.

It was a bad spot. Trouble had piled on trouble; it seemed we had reached the bottom. But the worst was yet to come.

The worst was—Gideon.

When Hallam Sperry walked out, leaving us under the watchful eyes of the squat toad named Brooks, Gideon was sitting motionless against the wall. He sat, still and rigid, for long moments, until I began to worry and said tentatively, "Gideon?"

He didn't answer. He sat staring, his face lined and fearful. I could almost see him shaking.

It was the worst shock of all to me: Gideon seemed to have lost his nerve entirely. I began to realize just how much I had depended on his strength and wisdom and patience—just then, when he was trembling on the point of collapse.

Things began to look very dark.

The "butler" noticed it and grinned. "They're all alike," he said contemptuously. "There won't be any trouble out of *him*. Or you either," he added, looking at me coolly.

I said, "The only trouble is what you make for yourself. You can't get away with this."

He said, "We can't?" He shook his head in mock worry. "Now you tell me," he said. "If you'd only mentioned it before——" I didn't laugh. I suppose I should have; because his imitation good humor vanished and, before I could dodge, I caught his clublike hand across the side of my head. I went reeling.

I barely heard him say, "That's for nothing. Now don't do anything!"

I shook my head and got up on hands and knees. At the Academy we had had, of course, plenty of training in hand-to-hand combat; if I could only have counted on Gideon to distract the man for a moment, I would have jumped him and taken my chances—even though he outweighed me two to one, and the weight was all animal muscle. But Gideon was still sitting frozen behind me, not even noticing what was going on. I said thickly:

"Brooks, you'll pay. You've got us, but sooner or later somebody's going to catch up with you, and you won't be carrying a gun."

"Gun?" he demanded contemptuously. "Who needs a gun?" He patted his pocket. "There it is and there it stays; if I can't take care of two miserable specimens like you with my bare hands I'll go back to Alcatraz and pound rocks to toughen up." He came closer and stood over me menacingly. "On your feet, little man," he ordered. "I haven't had my workout this morning, and I'll be glad to accommodate you if you want exercise. Sperry won't mind —it'll just soften you up for the brainpump later on."

The brainpump! So that was what was in store for us.
. . .

"Come on," he said thickly, his eyes glowing. He was an animal from skull to thick-booted feet, a creature of violence who loved his way of life. It looked like hard times for me; my only hope was to get up and take it, and pray for a quick knockout—

I pushed myself to my feet and leaped at him. It was

like jumping a Tiger tank—I went spinning away at the end of one of his giant fists. He laughed and came after me; I bounced off the wall and came in. . . .

And then Gideon moved.

Like a bolt of dark lightning he leaped from his seat and landed on the big man's back. I came in again, but I caught a random blow from Brooks' fist that sent me to the floor, dazed; I could only watch the two of them for a moment, while my muscles would not obey me. They were an uneven match—Gideon a little taller than the apeman, but at least fifty pounds lighter. After the first surprise, Brooks simply grunted and heaved and Gideon went flying; the butler lumbered after him and caught him around the throat. Those enormous muscles were choking the life out of Gideon; I crouched there, paralyzed, fighting with my own body to get up, to help Gideon. . . .

But Gideon needed no help. The hard days in Kelly's Kingdom had taught him more tricks than ever we learned at the Academy. I couldn't even see just what happened; all I saw was Gideon slumping, bringing his knees up under him; then an enormous surge of strength, and the squat man flying, Gideon after him and on him; a brief and savage scramble as the butler went for his gun. . . .

And then Gideon, bleeding and breathless, standing over him, holding the gun.

"Get up now, Jim," Gideon panted. "We're going to take a little walk."

16

Father Neptune: Farmhand

We got out of there—somehow.

I was only conscious of Gideon leading the way, the butler sullenly coming along, unlocking doors, keeping an eye open for other members of Sperry's staff. We were lucky; no one intercepted us. The butler, of course, was even luckier, for Gideon was right there with the gun.

We took the butler along for company as far as the express elevator banks, then we plunged in and left him standing there, just as the elevator doors closed.

We were in a hurry.

Gideon gripped my arm warningly; there were other passengers in the car; this was not the place to discuss our plans. We went down and down, to the bottom level of warehouses, before Gideon tugged at me and led me out of the elevators. Down a long, damp corridor, through a side passage, and I began to hear the rushing sounds of water.

We were back in Gideon's hermit-hideaway, on the ledge that overlooked the rushing drains. "All right, boy," said Gideon exultantly, "let them try to find us here!"

All the comforts of home. Even Gideon's little store of supplies and firewood still was intact; he busied himself starting a fire and setting a pot of water on it for his favorite steaming tea, while I tried to sort things out in my mind.

I said, "I don't understand it, Gideon. Brand Sperry shouldn't be here. He should be at the Academy."

"The old man must have called him home," said Gideon.

"But he can't! I mean, if Sperry left in the middle of a year, that would wreck his chances of graduating. And——"

"And maybe he doesn't care, boy." Gideon solemnly handed me a tin cup of tea; I set it down hastily and blew on my fingers. "Maybe the Academy looks like mighty small potatoes to the Sperrys right now. Something big is up, mark my words." He looked at me thoughtfully over the top of his own can of tea as he sipped it—he must have had asbestos lips! "Figure it out," he said. "One, you were followed all the way from the United States to Marinia. Those were Sperry's men—do you think they were doing it for fun? Two, one of those same men tried to kill you. Do you think that was just a joke? Three, somebody went to the trouble of trying to impersonate you here—nearly killing you in the process. That's getting to be a pretty bad joke by now, Jim!"

"But why?"

Gideon set down his tea and rubbed his chin thoughtfully, looking at me. "What was your uncle looking for in Eden Deep, Jim?" he inquired.

"Why—uranium."

"Uranium." He nodded, his soft eyes sober. "Uranium. And what is it that the whole world is short of now? So short that they have to cut down on power consumption everywhere—so short that the man who had control of a big new uranium lode would pretty near be able to write his own ticket? Uranium! Uranium's power—and power is what Hallam Sperry loves most of anything in the world."

I said, "But, Gideon, a man like Hallam Sperry doesn't have to do that! He's powerful now—rich, influential. He's the mayor of Marinia, he has shipping lines and submarine mines and all kinds of properties, more than any man needs."

"Why?" Gideon pursed his lips. "I don't know if I can tell you, Jim. You'd have to look inside Hallam Sperry's mind to know the answer, and to tell the truth that's not a job I'd much like—not without a brainpump, anyhow. Power's a disease; the more you get, the sicker you are; and Hallam Sperry's about as sick as he can be. Marinia? That's nothing to him, Jim!"

"But——"

"But nothing, Jim." He got up and rummaged in the crevices of the wall for the blankets he had neatly and methodically stowed away. "I don't know if you've noticed it, but it's pretty late and we've had a hard day. Let's get a night's sleep. Maybe we can find out some of the answers in the morning."

I slept, all right—but not easily. All night long I tossed and turned, dreaming of the Sperrys and my uncle and the man in the white suit and, most of all, that room with the brainpump and the body of Catroni.

I woke up, and Gideon was gone.

I searched the tunnel ledge all up and down its length without finding him; it was a bad twenty minutes. Then I heard cautious footsteps approaching; I got out of sight until the man coming toward me appeared . . . and it was Gideon.

He grinned at me. "Up so early, Jim?" he greeted me. "Thought you'd be sleeping for an hour yet."

"Where have you been?" I demanded. "I thought——"

"You thought old Hallam Sperry had come down here personally and snatched me away, did you? No, not this time, Jim. I just had a little business to attend to, that's all." He put down a knapsack and said: "Breakfast. We'll cook it up and eat, and then we'll pay a call on a friend of mine. Maybe he'll have some information for us."

We ate quickly enough, but then Gideon insisted on sitting and resting for a while, to my irritation. He calmed me down quickly enough, though—"Trust in Gideon," he said. "I've got a friend of mine out digging up information; give him time to get it done. We're safer here than we will be out there, anyhow. And more comfortable, too."

"More comfortable" was right. When finally Gideon decided it was time to move, he led me through byways and passages that I hadn't dreamed existed, to parts of Thetis I had never seen. We came out in a broad, high-ceilinged chamber, where the floor was a slimy trickle of greenish liquid and the air smelled of sour seaweed and iodine. Gideon stopped at the entrance and murmured, "Ever wonder what a place like Thetis is good for, Jim? Here's the answer, right in front of your eyes!"

All across the floor were stacks of sodden kelp and other marine vegetable growths. They were on raised platforms, a few inches above the floor of the chamber; from them liquid trickled and ran off, contributing to the dampness underfoot. "This is the draining chamber," Gideon whispered. "What they harvest in the farms outside comes in here; it's stacked and drained, and baled and sent to the processing chambers."

"It smells pretty fierce," I said.

Gideon chuckled. "Try and stand it for a few minutes," he advised. "I'll be back."

He left me standing there while he walked cautiously across the wide chamber and out of sight. No one else was around; I heard distant voices, but evidently the draining room didn't require much in the way of workmen.

I didn't have long to wait. I heard someone coming—fast. It was Gideon. As he drew near he panted, "Come on, Jim. We've got to get out of here! Sperry's got the whole city looking for us—we've got to leave fast!"

I followed almost without thinking, back the way we had come, through the back ways and secret passages Gideon knew so well. As we trotted along he filled me in: "Had a friend of mine checking up on what was going on," he panted. "Trouble, Jim! Sperry's captive police force—they're after us. Shoot on sight are the orders!"

"But he can't!"

"Jim, he can do anything! He's the mayor—he's the law in Thetis. You and me, we're just nobodies. We've got to get out of Thetis right away."

"But where can we go?"

"The ocean, boy! Where else? Where would your uncle go when he was in trouble? The Deeps!"

I said stumblingly, "But surely, Gideon, surely we can go to the officials here and straighten everything out. Sperry can't tear up the law!"

"He can sure try," Gideon panted grimly. "Boy, don't you understand yet? Sperry *is* the law in Thetis. We've got to fight him sooner or later, yes, but not this way. Our word against his—we'd be laughed out of court. You don't even have a passport, remember! You'd be picked up the minute you walked into a police station—if you lived to get that far!"

I shook my head. I said stubbornly, "What's the use of trying to get away? We'd get about as far as the gangway of one of Sperry's liners, and——"

Gideon grinned. "Who said anything about a liner?" he demanded. "Come on!"

He led the way. I followed, doubting—but what else was there to do? Twice we dodged into alleyways as the scarlet uniforms of the sea-police came into sight. It was unlikely that they were looking for us—but we couldn't take chances.

At last we came to a desolate tangle of grimy tunnels, where the sub-sonic pounding of mighty engines throbbed. It was the main pumping station for Thetis' drains—the point, perhaps, where I would have been caught in the suction and cast out into the crushing deep if Gideon hadn't plucked me from the stream. He said:

"Quiet, now. We're about to break a few laws."

He led the way through a narrow tunnel to a chamber lit by a single flickering Troyon tube. It was occupied by an elderly man, half asleep, his head bobbing on his breast; the room was lined with what seemed to be racks of diving gear. We paused at the entrance, Gideon silent as a wandering ghost, as he stared thoughtfully at the old man. Then, still silent, he shook his head and drew me back along the passage.

"Can't take a chance," he whispered. "The watchman would have the police on us in two minutes; we'll have to try the other port."

"To do what?" I demanded.

"To steal a pressure suit, Jim," he said. "What did you think? We're going out into the ocean."

I said, "Gideon, that's crazy. Where can we go? We can't get to another city in a pressure suit—we'd be picked up there just as easily as here if we did. Let's go back to the upper levels and——"

"And turn ourselves right over to Sperry, is that it? Jim, sometimes I wonder what they taught you in the Sub-Sea Academy! Just leave it to me, Jim. We'll get ourselves a couple of suits, and we'll sneak out to the farm belt. Chances are we'll be able to borrow a seacar there; if we do, we'll head for Seven Dome. Don't worry about us being picked up in Seven Dome—we'll take our chances. All clear? Now let's go get the suits. We can't get them here, with that watchman; we'll have to try the other port."

I thought, hard. "Well," I said, surrendering, "you know best, I suppose. Why can't we tie the watchman up, though? There is only one of him and there are two of us; we can——"

"Jim!" Gideon's expression was exasperated. "That's the *main pump station*. Suppose there should be a breakdown after we go, with the watchman tied up? Thetis would be drowned out, boy! Look, do me a favor. Quit thinking. Just come along!"

I came. Glumly.

But it seemed to be working out, I had to admit. The other port was not, for the moment, tended—the watchman was presumably off making his rounds. We found a pair of Edenite pressure suits that fitted us, gave their armor circuits a quick charge, slipped into the exit lock and sealed it.

The water boiled in around us, splashing against the steel baffles like 50-millimeter machine-gun shells against an armor plate. Even the splattering drops were almost violent enough to knock me off my feet; but it was only a few moments until the chamber was filled, pressure up to the outside intensity.

We opened the outer port, and climbed down a metal ladder to the sea floor.

The muck was almost knee deep. Gideon gesticulated—we were too close to Thetis to use our helmet talkers—and I managed to understand that he wanted me to adjust the suit's buoyancy tanks as he did. By juggling them, we reduced our effective weight to a couple of pounds—enough to keep us from floating off into the miles of empty water overhead, but little enough so that we could walk on top of the mud instead of sinking into it.

We tiptoed along on top of the muck like slow-motion ballet dancers. It was almost like those training periods at the bottom of the shallow Caribbean tidal waters. Secure in the armor my uncle had invented and given to the world, we had no feeling of the crushing pressure outside, no sense of the towering miles of water overhead. Here the muck was absolutely barren, barren and dark. The lights of Thetis behind us gave enough illumination for us to keep in touch with each other—we could not, of course, use helmet lights for fear of being spotted from a port. Once or twice the glimmering lights of a sub-sea liner slipped silently past overhead; other than that the dark was absolute.

For half an hour we flitted across the wasteland before topping a little submarine ridge. We saw ahead the waving streamers of kelp, the lights and structures of the subsea farms that surrounded Thetis.

The "kelp" was only distantly related to the seaweed of the old surface Sargasso, of course. It was a thick-stemmed, avidly growing vegetation that fed on the wastes from Thetis and the glow of floating batteries of Troyon tubes, where no other vegetation had grown since time began. There were many varieties of the seaweed, in every color of the spectrum, in every size from tiny mosslike growths to huge, thickbodied things that stretched a score of yards into the chill waters. Some were for food, some for fuel; many were for neither of those, but were living osmotic mining machines, capable of extracting pure elements from the sea water around them. These were the most miraculous of all—for they made it possible to harvest the suspended salts of the sea, drawing out the magnesium, iron, gold, silver—all the countless minerals that the deep sea waters held. They were as efficient as natural kelp was at extracting iodine, which so amazed the early chemists; but, of course, they had their limitations. And some few metals—uranium, the most important of them—did not exist in sea water in quantities large enough to matter, so that we were forced to rely on the mines. . . .

At once I was thinking of my uncle Stewart, under a mountain of water at the bottom of Eden Deep, because of Hallam Sperry. The faceplate of my pressure suit misted—

Gideon thumped my back, bringing his headpiece close to mine, and turned his helmet talker on to low power. "See that building?" He pointed to a group of lights half-hidden by the waving kelp. "That's where they keep the sea-cars. Because this is a sub-sea fleet base as well as one of Sperry's farms, it'll be guarded. But stick with me, Jim, and we'll make it."

He led the way; I followed. The growth was thick, occasionally we had to stop and hack ourselves free from the entangling growth with the sea-knives from our knee-scabbards. Far off to the right, harvesting machines floated through the water, clutching at the tangled kelp and gathering it into bales for transportation into the city, and eventual processing. Harvest was not a season but a year-round event in these farms, where the sun never dreamed of touching; after the harvest machines came cultivators and seeders, and a new crop was growing almost before the old one was inside the ports of Thetis.

We were lucky—we were not seen, though sea-cars floated by within scant yards of us, though a score and more of men in pressure-suits were moving about in the kelp jungles around us. If anyone caught a glimpse of us, no doubt he dismissed us as merely another pair of workers; but, so careful was Gideon in leading me through the concealing growths, I suspect we were never spotted at all.

At any rate, we reached the entrance port of the building around which the sea-cars nuzzled without challenge.

There was no question of talking now, of course; I had

only the waving of Gideon's arms to guide me. We crept up on the entrance port and stopped. He peered around, then worked the port controls. There was a rolling motion in the water around us as the powerful little pumps balanced the inside and outside pressure; then the port opened, we stepped into the lock and closed the outer door.

The water level began at once to fall.

If we had come in a sea-car we would certainly have been hailed and spotted. But you can hardly blame those sub-sea workers for keeping a slipshod watch on the port. A sea-car would have been detected by microsonar, and a dozen alarms would have called attention to it; but we, sneaking invisibly through the kelp, were in the sonar's blind spot, and there was of course no reason for suspecting that anyone would be stupid enough to come across the sea-bottom on foot. Nor, in truth, was there much reason to do so. There was nothing of value at the farms, except for the sea-cars themselves and the complex farming machinery—and those were pretty bulky objects for anyone to steal.

And yet, that was exactly what Gideon had in mind.

As soon as the water was out of the port chamber and the inner doors open, he strode out with assurance, leading me across the entrance chamber. There were men in sight, operating communications equipment, moving about in the corridors, perhaps half a dozen or more; but they hardly glanced at us. As though he knew every inch of the layout well (and, in fact, he did—for Gideon had worked in many a layout like this, with my uncle and otherwise—in his long sub-sea life), Gideon headed for the suit room. We shed our suits there; fortunately no one was in the room.

Then we stole a sea-car.

It was astonishingly easy—up to a point. With Gideon leading the way, we marched openly through the winding corridors of the farm administration building to the entry ports where the little sea-cars lay nuzzled. Then we became less open. Gideon spotted a small office; when no one was looking, we slipped into it and waited, listening.

The ready room was just outside our door, where the sea-car operators filed their reports and got their orders. Traffic was erratic; at times there seemed to be a dozen men in the room, and a few moments later it might be nearly empty.

We listened to their conversation, trying to judge which sea-car would be easiest to slip into, which held sufficient reserves of fuel for the trip to Seven Dome. There were remarks that puzzled me; it seemed that one of the sea-cars was special, in some way unlike the others.

A dawning idea began to grow in my mind. I nudged Gideon excitedly, but he hushed me. "Wait," he whispered. "They're all leaving. . . ."

The group of operators, talking among themselves, went out of the room on some unknown errand. It looked like our chance; Gideon gestured to me, and the two of us started to tiptoe out of the little office, into the ready room beyond which the sea-cars lay waiting. . . .

"*James Eden!*" crackled a familiar voice from behind us.

I spun around. There against the other door to the little office stood a tall youth in civilian clothing. He looked familiar, yet somehow wrong. As I stared at him I seemed to see, on his head, the flat scarlet cap of the Sub-Sea Academy, hear the echo of his voice flatly and contemptuously going over me back on the steps of Fletcher Hall.

Brand Sperry!

Gideon was quicker than I. He still had the gun we had taken from Sperry's "butler"; it was in his hand, and the younger Sperry was staring into its muzzle, before I had quite realized who it was. "Keep quiet, Sperry," Gideon whispered softly and dangerously. "If you want to stay alive, keep quiet."

Brand Sperry stopped as he was about to turn. He looked us over coolly. "What do you want?" he demanded.

I took a deep breath. I had had an idea, the ghost of a thought, listening to the sea-car operators talk; it seemed to me that there was a bare possibility that the "special" sea-car was special indeed. After all, Hallam Sperry had claimed to have something very special in the way of sea-cars, back in the room where Catroni lay dead. . . .

I said: "We want my uncle's experimental job, Sperry. We know it's here. Where is it?"

Gideon was a champion; he gave me one quick look, and then backed me up: "That's right, Sperry! Hurry up!" But he must have thought, for a moment, that I was out of my head.

But I wasn't. Brand Sperry's piercing eyes flamed and he snapped: "Eskow! He tipped you off! That little——"

"Shut up, Sperry!" Gideon said sharply. "You don't want to attract any attention here—you'll be the first one hurt!"

"Wait a minute, Gideon," I said. "What's this about Eskow?"

"You know," Brand Sperry sneered. "I told my father. I knew it was a mistake bringing him here. We kept your message from getting to him the first time, but I knew you'd reach him sooner or later—and I knew he'd spill everything he knew to you!"

I said, "Sperry, I haven't seen Eskow except through the viewport at the docks. Not that it makes any difference. Where is he?"

Sperry shrugged. "Last I saw, he was in the ready room a couple of hours ago. My father transferred him off the liner because he thought we might get information out of him about you. I warned him!"

I stared at Gideon pleadingly, but he read my mind. "No, Jim," he said. "We haven't got time to look up old friends. Any minute someone might walk in on us, and then where will we be? You, Sperry—we want that sea-car. Take us to it!"

"I'll do no such thing," Sperry said frostily—and for a moment there, I almost admired him; he might have had a squad of sea-police at his back as he confronted us. "Put that gun down. I'll have the guards take care of you two——"

Gideon kept his grin. He said gently, "Mr. Sperry, I don't advise you to make any trouble. I really don't."

Abruptly his tone changed to a crackle: "You young idiot!" he blazed. "Jim Eden and I were *that* close to being brain-pumped by your father. We know that he sank Jim's uncle—tried to kill Jim half a dozen times—we know that every dirty deal and corrupt official in Marinia belongs to him. Do you think I'd hesitate to shoot *you* if you give me half a chance? Get a move on, man! Take us to Eden's sea-car—*now!* And thank your lucky stars I don't shoot you dead this minute!"

Brand Sperry saw the light of reason.

He conducted us to the sea-car, conscious of the gun in Gideon's pocket. He sharply ordered the dispatcher to mind his own business when the man appeared and started to ask a question. Heaven knows what the dispatcher thought—but he had undoubtedly learned, working for the Sperry interests, that it didn't pay to get in the way of anyone named Sperry.

Sperry strode stiffly before us into the entrance hatch of the sea-car, never looking back. We followed him.

And then the three of us were inside, and the vessel was sealed, and cast loose from the little dome.

We were free!

"Smart work, Jim," Gideon acknowledged. "I heard what the operators were saying, but it never occurred to me that this was that first sea-car your uncle built. That makes it yours, I guess—so we aren't even stealing it!"

"We'll see what the law says about that!" snapped Brand Sperry, his voice rising. "You men are thieves, plain and simple!"

Gideon only looked at him, and gestured gently with the gun; Brand Sperry was silent—but fuming.

Gideon turned the controls over to me, and I set course for Seven Dome. He stood over my shoulder, thoughtfully watching, until I grew uneasy and said: "Isn't that where you want us to go, Gideon? Seven Dome? You said——"

"I know what I said, Jim," he agreed hesitantly. "Only ——"

"Only what?"

He looked around him, at the inside of the sea-car. It

looked much like any other—perhaps there was a slightly brighter glimmer from the Edenite armor, to show that it was stronger, more powerfully charged, than most. Gideon said:

"This one has the same kind of armor as the one your uncle Stewart was lost in, doesn't it?"

"I guess so," I agreed.

"So it ought to be able to take quite a lot of pressure, right?"

But this time I was used to Gideon's long and complicated way of getting at anything he had to say; I only nodded without trying to rush him.

He said, striking off in another direction, "You remember what we saw in the reel that was brainpumped from Catroni?" I nodded, and he went on: "Sure you do. After Catroni pulled out, a man followed him. Only the other man's armor had been sabotaged; it couldn't take the pressure, and he was killed."

"That's right, Gideon. My uncle."

"Was it?" Gideon demanded sharply. "We've been thinking it was, sure—but how did we know? There was another man on board, after all—Westervelt, the engineer."

I said slowly, "You mean the man who was killed might not have been my uncle?"

"That's right, Jim." Gideon's dark face was sober as he looked at me. "Now, it's only a guess—don't get your hopes up! Even if that first one was Westervelt, your uncle might have tried a little later in another suit, if he could patch one together—or the sea-car's armor might have failed over the weeks he's been down there, or he might have run out of air—— Oh, it's only an outside chance. But what if he's still alive at the bottom of Eden Deep, Jim?"

I looked at him for a long moment. Then I returned to the controls and sent the little sea-car heeling over as I swung it around.

"We're going to find out!" I said. "Or we'll sink ourselves trying!"

17

Into the Deeps

We made a curious crew, the three of us, as we bored through the cold, dense waters toward Eden Deep.

Brand Sperry, after the first few minutes, sat himself down in the navigator's seat and stared unseeingly at the blackness outside. He didn't offer conversation; for my part, I was glad to have him quiet.

Fortunately, we knew my uncle's position when Catroni scuttled the ship. I could still see, through Catroni's eyes, the entire instrument panel; if the Academy had taught me anything, it had taught me to read the gauges and meters on the control board of any sub-sea vessel in a single sweeping glance. I would have no more trouble putting us right over the hulk of my uncle's sea-car than I would in finding my way across my bedroom at the Academy in the dark.

The trip, I estimated, would take us another hour and a half. I put the controls on auto; but I was too eager to get up from the pilot's seat and let the sea-car take itself to the gridpoint. I sat there, watching the distance gauge whirl slowly through its arc, watching the miles reel past, almost unable to keep my hands off the diving rudders and the stabilizers, though I knew perfectly well that the autopilot would do a far better job of keeping the little car on course than any mere human.

Gideon said: "Tired, Jim? Want to take a little nap?"

I shook my head. "I couldn't sleep," I said. "But if you want to——"

"Neither could I." Pause, while Brand Sperry stared stonily into nothingness. Gideon said, "Are you sure you can take us to Stewart's sub?"

I shrugged. "I can put us right over it, I'll guarantee. Getting down—that's something else. All I can do is dive the car; whether or not it will take the pressure is something I don't know. Don't forget, Gideon, that this is the *first* experimental sea-car my uncle built. Maybe it's as strong as the other—maybe not."

Gideon nodded slowly. "Well," he said, "we'll find out——"

That seemed to cover that.

We plunged on through the dark waters. The little motors of the sea-car whined almost inaudibly, the hissing friction of the waters sliding along the Edenite armor whispered in our ears, the slow, erratic clicking of the autopilot and the instruments lulled me. There were other noises, too—

I realized, abruptly, that some of the other noises didn't belong there.

I sat up straight, listening. From somehwere in the sea-car there came a faint, furtive scratching. It stopped; in a moment I heard it again.

Gideon heard it too. I caught the look of sudden tension in his eyes as we both got the same idea at the same time. . . .

Someone else was in the sea-car!

Gideon looked a wordless threat at Brand Sperry—who paid him no attention—and silently, holding the captured gun, Gideon stepped to the door to the after compartment. Fools, to have forgotten to search the little sub! I blamed myself angrily.

Gideon flung the door open, peered in, then lunged inside and I heard a scramble of motion.

In a moment Gideon appeared again, frowning. "Jim,"

he groaned, "we ought to be kicked. Look who was here,
at the aft communicator—heaven knows what messages
he was sending!"

He gestured with the gun, and another figure stepped
uncertainly through the doorway—

Bob Eskow!

I said, "Bob!"

He stared at me. "I—I thought it was you, Jim," he
said. "I couldn't believe it! Jim Eden—a thief!"

The expression on his face was impossible to read.
Gideon said sharply, "Young man, Jim Eden is no more a
thief than—"

I stopped him. I said, "Bob, listen to me. You've got to
trust me." As quickly as I could I told him everything
that had happened since I came to Marinia—our hopes of
finding my uncle's ship, the duplicity of the Sperrys, the
threat to our lives. It was a long story, short as I tried to
make it, and I couldn't tell if he was believing me as I
spoke. When I finished he sighed and looked at the floor.

"I—I don't know, Jim," he said wearily. "It's pretty
hard to take in. I admit—well, I knew something was
wrong. When I saw you at the landing stages and you ran
away—"

"Bob! I didn't run away! I tried to see you—I sent a
message—they told me you didn't want to talk to me."

He stared at me grimly. "I got no message," he said.
"You see? I can look at that either way—either you ran,
or what you say is true, and the Sperry gang kept me from
seeing you." He shook his head. "How can I tell? When
you came aboard this ship I was giving it a pre-cruise
inspection. I thought it was you, Jim, and it was a hard
thing for me to make up my mind what to do. The only
solution I could come to was to message Thetis, tell them
what happened, let them send a patrol sea-car after us and
bring you back. I thought the courts could decide, Jim.
. . ."

"The courts are Hallam Sperry," said Gideon.

Bob nodded slowly. "So you tell me," he said. "But
____"

A tiny bell was ringing, and it stopped that conversation right there. I jumped back to the controls. "We're over the gridpoint!" I cried. "If our computations were right—my uncle's sea-car is right below us!"

I cleared the auto-pilot with a swift touch of the keys and took over manual control. I hesitated, looking over my shoulder at Bob Eskow.

He nodded reluctantly. "We're this far," he said. "Go ahead, Jim. If your uncle's ship is down there—well, that answers a lot of questions. But Jim—don't forget that I messaged Thetis. A Sea Patrol car should be right on our tails!"

Gideon chuckled softly. "They'll have a sweet job following where we're going, boy," he said. "This is Eden Deep—seven and a half miles straight down. Drop her, Jim!"

I nodded and touched the controls. The buoyancy tanks began to fill as the tiny pumps droned and spurted sea-water into them. I set course for a wide circle, gently eased over the diving vanes. The clinometer showed three degrees dive, then five; then, carefully, I slipped the vanes to the full fifteen-degree crash dive position and opened up the propeller motors. . . .

And our little sea-car began clawing downward into Eden Deep.

Already we were close to the bottom limits of most sea-cars, even with standard Edenite armor. Nearly four miles of water towered over us; the pressure would have smashed steel, squeezed quartz like putty. As we went down and down, four and a quarter miles, and four and a half, I saw something that I never had seen before. At first I thought it was a trick of eyestrain—a faint glimmering twinkle of light on the walls of the cabin. But I saw it again, flickering like witch-fire, and it grew stronger, and I realized that it was the sparkling glow of the Edenite armor, showing on the inside of the hull, giving a faint notion of the enormous forces pressing against it, pressures that could destroy any metal and penetrate even the mighty strength of ordinary Edenite. . . .

Still we sank down.

At cruising speed we swept in a broad descending spiral, a thousand feet a minute. We were at five miles, then six, and the witch-fires on the inside of the hull were sparkling bright.

Brand Sperry was staring at them, his face a rigid mask. Gideon looked at him, then glanced at me warningly; Sperry was in an ecstasy of terror.

For that matter, there were strange tinglings along my own spine. I had never been this deep before—only three men had, or at least only three living men had reached it. Two were certainly dead—one instantly, in the fraction of a second after his suit failed; the other more lingeringly, under Hallam Sperry's brainpump. The third was my uncle, the inventor of the flickering force armor that was all that kept the water out . . . and he had done it, I reminded myself, in the ship he had built *after* constructing this first pilot model. . . .

What improvements had he found it necessary to make? There was no way to know—no way to guess whether this armor was going to hold.

Even Edenite armor cannot accept the giant pressure of six miles of water without showing signs of strain. It was only a faint metallic *ping*, the sound of straining metal under any circumstances, so tiny that under normal circumstances none of us would even have heard it—but it brought all of us straight up, eyes wide, faces taut, waiting for the hammering rush of the torrent.

It didn't come; it had been only a noise and nothing more. But it cracked Brand Sperry. He cried desperately, "Stop! Eden—stop this! Take us back up—you're killing us!" He glared at me wildly; I opened my mouth to answer—but he was springing at me. I half dodged away.

But Gideon was there before me. As Brand Sperry scrambled past him Gideon brought up his fist and caught him right behind the ear; Sperry went over without a sound, sprawled on the deck, unconscious.

The three of us stared at him wordlessly.

At last Gideon cleared his throat. "Boy," he rumbled, "that young pirate raises a question in my mind. You and me, Jim, we know what we're doing; this is a risk we've got to take, and I'm not looking for a way out of it. But what about Sperry and your friend Bob, here? It isn't their risk, Jim."

I swallowed—it wasn't easy. The temptation to say enthusiastically, "Sure, Gideon!" and send the sea-car up again as fast as its propellers could drive was almost overpowering. For the flickering on the inside of the Edenite armor was a dazzling blur of color now; I could hear a symphony of tiny metallic creaks and squeals as the armor settled under its load; I had all too vivid a picture in my mind of the Edenite charge leaking off the armor under the stress of the pressure, and the sea thundering in to destroy us.

I looked at Bob Eskow. He was the calmest of us all. His face was like something carved out of sea-basalt; he said:

"Keep going, Jim."

Six and a half miles.

Seven. I came out of a half stupor, tore my eyes from the clicking, purring depth gauge, switched on the scanning drive of the microsonar. Faint spots of color began to appear in its viewplate, nothing recognizable as yet.

Gideon's voice was very quiet. "Jim," he said softly, but with a note that snatched my eyes off the viewplate. "Look at the floor."

From the after compartment, through the door, came trickling a thin, lazy line of water.

18

The Bottom of the World

Training counts for a great deal.

I think that if it had not been for the years of constant pounding and discipline in the Academy—*Panic is the enemy!*—I would have cracked right then and there; I would have manhandled the little sea-car straight up, crash-blasted the ballast out of the tanks, lost control and most likely killed us all.

But some little voice inside me, something that had more wit than I, stopped me, told me that the picture was somehow *wrong*. I held off wrenching the controls to full-climb for a fraction of a second.

And in that fraction of a second I understood. At seven miles, sea-water doesn't *trickle*. What made that thin line of water I didn't know—but it wasn't, it couldn't be, a leak.

I jumped up from the controls, leaving them locked in position, and raced back to the after compartment. There, lacking occupants and therefore lacking heat, the walls were icy cold; moisture was condensing on them; it was that moisture that had trickled in.

I went back to my seat more slowly. I told Bob and Gideon what it was. Neither of them said a word.

Brand Sperry was beginning to stir. Gideon stood close

to him, one eye still on Bob, but ready to handle Sperry if he still wanted fight. There was no fight in him, though; he opened his eyes, looked at me once, and then lay staring at the ceiling.

I went back to my controls.

And on the microsonar screen was a tiny, torpedolike shape, its outline blurred and half drowned out by bottom-return, but easy enough to recognize. It could be nothing else; it had to be my uncle's ship.

The armor held.

We gently, prayerfully, settled down atop the other sea-car; there was a gentle bump, and we were locked hull-to-hull.

That was as far as our planning had gone—if "planning" is the word for as frantic and harum-scarum a dash as Gideon and I had made from Thetis to Eden Deep. We were actually touching my uncle Stewart's ship—or his tomb.

What next?

Gideon and I looked at each other questioningly.

It was impossible for us to cross from one ship to another—we had no armor capable of standing these pressures. The armor in the sea-car was standard Edenite, like every other suit of depth armor on every other sea-car in the oceans; perfectly safe at four miles, even five—but not at seven and a half!

Gideon said, "The grapples, Jim."

I crossed my fingers; but I nodded. It was the only way. I coaxed our little sub into perfect alignment with the pattern of the other on the microsonar; then gently opened the rheostats to the magnetic grapples. It was quite a load to try on them; but it had to work. There was no alternative.

I started the ballast pumps, forcing a part of the water out of the buoyancy tanks—not too much, for too much strain on the grappling magnets would break our grip for sure. Then, gently, I rocked the two linked sea-cars back and forth with the drive propellers. . . .

It was a strange thing, but in shallow water it would

have been impossible. Here it was—almost—but not quite.

In shallow water there would have been currents and turbulence; the scouring of the water flow would have heaped silt around my uncle's sea-car, half buried it. I never could have broken the suction of hundreds of tons of mud.

But at the bottom of Eden Deep, the water lay dead and cold. There were no currents—it is heat that makes currents in the water, just as it is the sun's heat that makes the winds of the air, and here, nearly forty thousand feet down, the sun's heat never reached. There had been some slight disturbance from the coming to rest of the sea-car itself; but the suction was not great; and it was only a few moments before we were free.

We were free!

I set course for a steep, ascending curve, to top the ridges that surround Eden Deep, en route to Thetis.

Thetis was our destination—but Thetis was out of reach.

Long before we topped the ridge, while we were still hundreds of fathoms below the normal cruising depth, we ran into the first signs of trouble.

It was only a flickering shadow on the very rim of the microsonar—a shadow that split and wavered, and joined again, and divided to become three shadows.

The Sea Patrol!

Bob Eskow said miserably, "My fault, Jim. I called them."

I shook my head. "You did what you thought was right, Bob. The question is, what do we do now?"

"Give up," snarled Brand Sperry. Now that we were out of the Deep itself, he seemed to have recovered his nerve. "You're beaten, you know. I don't care what you find in your uncle's sub—you can't stand up against my father!"

We ignored him. Gideon said meditatively, "Looking at the charts, I notice something. We're only about fifty miles from Fisherman's Island, Jim. Your uncle used to have a post there—used it for air transport connections, back in the days when he had mining operations all over this area. I believe the island is deserted now—it's just a tiny thing, with a coral reef; never had any native population."

Bob said, "What about it? What good would that do us?"

Gideon shrugged. "We might perhaps hole up there for a while," he suggested. "And—well, I don't know about you, Mr. Eskow. But I'm pretty sure Jim and I are anxious to get inside Stewart Eden's sea-car as quickly as we can." He didn't say why—but I knew without his mentioning it what he had in mind. Neither of us wanted to mention it, neither of us dared voice the hope aloud—

But we didn't know for *sure* that Uncle Stewart was dead.

Gideon pointed out the advantages to his scheme: The route to Fisherman's Island was almost perfect for our needs. We could hug the slope of the ridge for half the distance, well below the usual cruising depth of sea-cars, almost certainly beyond range of detection (since micro-sonar equipment had its limitations, one of which was that scanning *downward* was harder than scanning *upward*, due to reflection-return from the sea bottom). And even when we breasted the ridge, the bottom at that point was covered with peaks and guyots; we could slip through the valleys between them, and only the wildest chance would let the Sea-Patrol spot us.

The trip took less than two hours, in spite of our serpentine wanderings among the submarine peaks. The ranging Sea Patrol cars were constantly in our sonar screen; but always at extreme range. I was certain they never detected us.

We circled around the underwater slopes that surfaced as Fisherman's Island, and I headed for the surface. At a depth of only a few yards, operating on the sonar plate, I found the channel to the lagoon inside the coral reef, threaded the passage, the captive sea-car clutched beneath us in the grapples clearing the bottom by scant feet in places, and surfaced a few hundred feet from shore.

It was the first time I had been on the surface in—was it only weeks? It seemed like years!

I spun the upper hatch open and poked my head out, ready to be blinded by the sun.

There wasn't any sun. Overhead the sky was a powder of white. It was night time; the stars were infinite and brilliant; the water was flickering with luminous life; the shore was dead dark. I had forgotten, almost, that there were such things as night and day!

I quickly checked my chronometer: it was an hour or so before sunrise. Looking hard at the horizon, I thought I could see the beginning of a faint violet glow.

"Let's get to work," said Gideon.

It took us an hour to jockey my uncle's sea-car into position. With the help of every straining combination of grapples and hydraulic extensors, we succeeded in easing it out from under us, heaving it ahead of us onto the coral sand. The tide was high—as high as the gentle tides of the Pacific ever run—and the top of the sub's hull was just awash. We waited, then. For half an hour, then half an hour more, until the waterline had receded to just below the entrance port.

All four of us were standing atop the little sea-car's hull, waiting for the last licking wavecrest to fall below the lip of the port. Brand Sperry was haughty and still; Bob Eskow was plainly bone-tired. But Gideon and I were tense and eager, and it was all I could do to keep myself from opening the port prematurely.

Then we could wait no longer. We left Bob to watch over Brand Sperry; Gideon and I wrenched the port open and clattered inside. A cascade of water followed us as one large wave topped the port; but that was all.

Inside was fetid darkness. The hot, stale air was almost a poison; I found myself choking, heard Gideon's cough beside me. Gideon had been more foresighted than I: While I was staring around dazedly, trying to see in the gloom, there was a click and Gideon turned on a hand-light.

We were in the after compartment. Around us were

the signs of Catroni's treachery—wrecked equipment, smashed instruments, sabotaged engines. It would be a long, long time before this ship would be fit again.

But wreckage was not what we were looking for; we searched every corner of the after compartment with Gideon's flash, looking for some trace of my uncle—or the other man. There was no one, live or dead.

And there was no sound.

I think that that was the worst moment of all for me. To have salvaged the sea-car itself, in the face of everything, was so great a triumph that I had almost felt certain that we would find my uncle alive inside—I had known, somehow, just what it would be like to open the port and have my uncle, somehow alive and hearty, come chuckling out. . . .

Gideon touched my shoulder wordlessly. The two of us turned hopelessly toward the forward cabin.

There was no destruction here, at any rate—this was where my uncle and his friend had been, all unsuspecting, while Catroni murdered the ship. The darkness was blacker still. Gideon pierced it with his flash. . . .

Together we saw it: A heap of rags, huddled before the control panel, it seemed. We leaped forward, Gideon a half-step before me.

The face, pale and still, was the face of my uncle Stewart. The eyes were closed; there was not a trace of motion. Gideon bent over him with a half-smothered sound.

Time stood still. At last Gideon, his eyes huge, looked up at me.

"Glory be to God, Jim Eden," he said prayerfully. "He's alive!"

19

Back from the Dead

That was how my Uncle Stewart came back to us.

We got Bob Eskow to help us; the three of us managed to get him up through the tiny hatch, onto our own sea-car, into the light. Stewart opened his eyes and looked at me, and he smiled. But he had no strength to speak.

Once again the Academy helped me. Exhaustion, starvation and the poisonous effects of foul air were no strangers to the men of the Sub-Sea Fleet; and every semester, we had had drilled into us the methods of emergency treatment. From the little first-aid locker of the sea-car we took stimulants and elixirs and the miraculous chemical blends that were guaranteed to bring a near-corpse whooping back to life. Stewart needed them all. While I was mixing up a sugar solution for intravenous feeding, Gideon quickly injected a whole series of stimulating drugs, and Bob arranged the electric heart stimulator coils in position for quick use—if they were needed. We had found my uncle Stewart alive—and we were not going to let him go!

I don't know how long we worked over him. It must have been only half an hour or so—we hadn't the complicated equipment to take much longer—but time stopped. It might have been seconds, or years.

And time began to tick forward once more when the last injection was made, and the food solution was trickling into his veins, and my uncle Stewart opened his eyes once more.

They were sane eyes, wakeful eyes. They were the soberly humorous, warmly gay eyes I remembered from my childhood and the New London shore.

And Stewart whispered, with the old chuckling undertone:

"Hello, Jim."

In the wild excitement of that moment, can we be blamed for forgetting a couple of comparatively unimportant little things?

We propped Stewart up in the closest approach to comfort you can find in a sea-car. We bundled him in warm covers and tried to keep him as quiet as could be, and then, almost at once, we looked at each other with foolish surprise. For we had remembered something.

What had happened to Brand Sperry?

We left Gideon clucking over my uncle, and Bob and I raced for the other sea-car. It lay bobbing gently in the slacking tide, looking harmless and deserted.

As, indeed, it was. Brand Sperry was gone.

Bob and I looked out over the peaceful lagoon at Fisherman's Island. The peaceful look of the water was a lie. We knew that it was much less than peaceful; we had seen the triangular warning signals of sharks, we knew of the octopus lairs and the scores of other shallow-water perils that that harmless sparkling water concealed.

"If he wanted to get away that bad," said Bob Eskow, "I say let him go."

I nodded. "Especially since there isn't anything we can do about it!" I agreed. "We can't stay here forever. He's out of trouble, leave him alone."

We went back to our own sea-car, feeling relaxed and at ease for the first time, it seemed, in many months.

Stewart Eden was sitting up, and his eyes were bright. Gideon declared that he was strong enough to talk, if we didn't excite him too much. Stewart chuckled: "After the—

call it a rest cure—I've just gone through, I doubt you'll
excite me too much, Gideon. It was a' most restful time,
believe me. Plenty of sleep, plenty of idle hours. I had no
complaints on that score. . . ."

We pressed him for his story, but there was little he had
to tell. What we had plucked from dead Catroni's mind,
what we had surmised ourselves from the wrecked interior
of his sea-car—that was the story. There was nothing
much beside. Except—

"Uranium!" my uncle whispered, his eyes agleam and
fixed on something far beyond us all. "Thousands and
thousands of tons of the highest-grade ore, Jim! Just
scrape away the ooze, and there it is. Eden Deep is the
richest store of fissionable ore the world has ever seen, and
with my new Edenite it's there for the taking. We've
proved that!" He leaned back against the wall, panting
heavily. "It's power for the world; power to run every
machine that man can build for centuries to come. Cheap
power, power in quantities the world has never known."
He smiled, and almost as an afterthought he said: "Do you
know, Jim, that you will be very, very rich?"

I protested: "It isn't mine, Uncle Stewart! It's all yours.
You filed claim on Eden Deep; you invented the armor."

"And what good did it do me, while I was locked away
down there, watching the oxygen level go down? No,
Jim—it's not mine, it's for all of us. A share for you and a
share for me, yes—and shares for Gideon and Bob as
well. No need to be hoggish about this! There's plenty for
all of us. Why, we'll be walking on thousand-dollar bills,
Jim; we'll be richer than old Hallam Sperry ever was,
we'll——"

"Hallam Sperry," said Gideon thoughtfully. "Mr. Eden,
you have made me remember something. Excuse me." He
disappeared toward the control chamber; and, in a moment, we heard him grunt as though he had received a
blow.

He reappeared, his dark face furrowed. "Perhaps we
ought to hold off on the congratulations for a little while,"
he said. "They might be just a little bit premature. While
we're sitting around here, counting our money and decid-

ing how we're going to spend it, trouble's coming our way. And it's coming fast!"

I jumped to the microsonar, and Gideon's words came true before my eyes. A thin single trace across the blue, shining face of the instrument. It was another sea-car, not at extreme range but in close, not patrolling in easy curves, but vectored in on Fishermen's Island. There was only one explanation: Some time, somehow, Brand Sperry had found a moment unguarded at the communicators and sent an alarm. And his father's ship was on our trail!

"Secure all ports!" I bawled to Bob Eskow, and with the quick discipline of our days at the Academy he leaped to obey. Gideon jumped to the instruments, and I started the motors. We slipped out from the reef, under the surface of the water and down.

There was no hope of evasion this time. They had us spotted and dead to rights. We could flee; that was all.

As fast as the hard-driven engines could take us, we pounded through the clinging water, straight out in the Pacific deeps.

We slid through the water, deeper and deeper, for long minutes, while we watched the trace of the pursuers in the plates. They were not gaining on us perceptibly, but I knew that the time would come when luck would run out for us. Our little sea-car had been through a punishing ordeal; primitive and crudely wrought, it had been at the very limit of its endurance when we rescued my uncle; underpowered and never broken in, it had been pushed too far too long. If only we could stay ahead of them long enough to reach Thetis, or one of the other underwater cities! At least there we could hope to evade Sperry's thugs long enough to reach some high official, too high to have been bought by the power of Sperry's millions. . . .

But it was out of the question. It was a trip of many hours to the nearest of the cities. And we had, at the brutally high speeds we were using, no hope of averting a breakdown for that length of time.

"Go deep," said my uncle. "Perhaps we can bluff them."

I advanced the diving planes and blinked at him with the beginnings of hope. "Bluff?" I asked. "But that's no bluff, Uncle Stewart! You're right! We can avoid them forever that way! This ship will go clear to the bottom of Eden Deep—they'll never be able to touch us. We can——"

He was shaking his head. "No, Jim," he said. "Even at the bottom of Eden Deep, they'd just circle overhead, waiting for us. We would have to come up, some time, and there they would be. But it's worse than that. Look!"

He pointed to the bulkhead, where a fine dancing needle was feathering into the room. I stared at it, not recognizing what it was.

But Gideon recognized it. "We're leaking," he said, in a voice that tolled like the dirges of doom.

Stewart Eden nodded. In his dry whisper he said, "Leaking is right, and we're only a thousand fathoms down. If we had my own sea-car instead of this one— But we don't. We'll never see the bottom of Eden Deep, my boy. But the only hope we have is to persuade Sperry otherwise. . . ."

It was a desperate gamble, but it was all we could do.

The cards were all stacked Hallam Sperry's way. We watched the dancing feather of spray that came from the tiny leakage between the plates of our hull, and turned to the microsonar screen, where the little pip of light that marked the pursuers grew steadily closer, and wherever we looked there was no hope.

For a moment I thought we had a chance. The following pip darted upward toward the mass of Fisherman's Island. "They've lost us!" I thought. "They think we're still on the Island——"

But even while I thought it, I knew I was wrong. The pip hesitated only a matter of moments; then it came sliding down the side of the submarine mountain again, hot on our trail.

Hallam Sperry had stopped just long enough to pick up his son; it had delayed him bare minutes, and there would be no more delays.

At the end of one hour, the end was upon us.

My uncle Stewart was on his feet, ranging the little cabin of the sea-car, his voice hoarse and raging as he talked to the face of the microsonar. "You squids, you sea-urchins," he whispered, "You unblessed children of mangy devilfish! Ah, it gravels me to see you get your way, Hallam Sperry! Death I can face, but to see the likes of you running the world with the power I found—that hurts, Sperry, it hurts deep down!"

Gideon said soothingly, "Just sit down and rest, Mr. Eden. You'll wear yourself out like that."

"Wear myself out!" Stewart Eden's whisper crackled with passion. "I'll wear Sperry out, if I ever get my hands on him! Jim!"

I said automatically, "Yessir!"

"Jim, I promised you thousand-dollar bills to walk on, and I'm not going to be able to keep the promise. I'm sorry, boy. About all I can promise you right now is a sub-sea sailor's grave."

"That's good enough for me, Uncle Stewart," I said. "But I hate to see Hallam Sperry getting control of Eden Deep!"

Stewart Eden's fighting grin was on his lips. "If that's all that's bothering you, boy," he said in his whispering chuckle, "why, I can take care of that right now. Eskow, can you raise Thetis on the communicator?"

"Why—yes, sir. But they can't reach us in time——"

"Of course they can't. Get them on the communicator, that's all I ask." While Bob worked the controls of the deep-sea TBS, my uncle carefully printed a long message on the back of a chart of Eden Deep.

It took long minutes, while the pursuing shadow gained on the overloaded motors of our sea-car; but finally Bob raised his head and reported. "Contact with Thetis, sir," he sang out.

"Good enough," chuckled my uncle. "Here's the message."

Bob took it from him, scanning the first line. "There's no addressee, sir," he said. "Who shall I send it to?"

"Route it to all interested parties, boy! Don't wait—

you've got to get it out before Hallam Sperry catches up with us! One little ram from his sea-car and we'll open up like an oyster in Deep-Sea Dave's!"

Bob looked puzzled, but as his eyes traveled farther down the message he first stared disbelievingly, then grinned to match my uncle's lean, wolfish expression. "Aye-aye, sir!" he said joyously, and bent to the communicator.

I leaned over his shoulder as his racing fingers tapped out the message. It began:

"To whom it may concern. This is Stewart Eden calling. We are being pursued, and will shortly be rammed and sunk, by a sea-car operated by or under the control of Hallam Sperry, who was accomplice to the sabotage of my experimental very-deep sea-car which was sunk in Eden Deep. Sperry now has possession of one of the two existing models of a sea-car constructed of a new form of Edenite armor which makes it possible to attain any depth of water that exists anywhere on earth. With this armor, it will be possible to mine Eden Deep, at the bottom of which is located an enormous field of uranium ore. I, Stewart Eden, hereby give and transfer all of my right, title and interest in the process for manufacturing this new armor to the world at large, irrevocably and forever. The formula for manufacture is as follows: A generator capable of maintaining a K-87 magnetostriction field is connected in series to———"

The rest was technical. But the effect was plain:

My uncle Stewart had robbed Hallam Sperry of his super-Edenite by giving it to the world! Gone were the billions that his process would have brought him and me—gone perhaps were our very lives—but Hallam Sperry would not be able to exploit the Deeps singlehanded!

20

Duel in the Deeps

In the center of the microsonar screen was the hovering pip that was our own sea-car; the pursuer was so close that the two pips were actually touching in the screen.

Deep-sea subs are armed, but at the speeds we were using the arms were useless. There are torpedoes and submarine rockets and mines; but none of them can travel any faster than a full-speed sea-car, and at our depths, as close as we were to each other, any explosion that harmed us would destroy Hallam Sperry as well. The pure concussion would stove in the hulls of both vessels.

It was a matter of ramming that we had to fear, and it could be only seconds off.

My uncle Stewart, by now as fully recovered as though he had spent a month sunning himself under the Troyon lamps at Thetis, was handling the controls himself. He had built the sea-car; he could get every last knot out of the straining engines. But, drive them to their limit as he might, we couldn't gain a fathom on Sperry, hovering close behind. Each moment Sperry drew infinitesimally nearer; each second brought us that much closer to the gentle nudging jolt that would start our plates and send us spinning toward the ooze below.

We were too deep for safety already; Gideon and Bob Eskow were pounding caulking into the dozen splitting leaks at the joints of the hull—but under the pressures that were forcing their way through, the caulking came arrowing out as quickly as they could drive it in. We were fifteen hundred fathoms down—deeper than the safe range of a normal sea-car, at least twice as deep as we should have dared to take the limping, rickety hulk we were piloting.

There was no escape. There was nothing we could do. We couldn't even turn and fight. We could only keep running—hopelessly.

"Blast it all!" roared my uncle Stewart. "Gideon, Bob—I apologize to you for getting you into this. I don't have to apologize to you, Jim—we're the same blood; but it's not your fight, Bob. Or yours, Gideon."

Gideon grinned, the white teeth friendly. "It is now, captain," he said. "And Bob Eskow's too, I'd guess; I doubt that Hallam Sperry would let us surrender even if we wanted to."

Stewart Eden pounded the depth compass and sent its needle spinning crazily. "That's what I wanted to know!" he cried. "All right, boys; we'll call it one for all and all for one, eh? It's no hope I'm giving you—there isn't any hope. But if we're going to drown, I'm going to drown a couple of Sperrys along with us! Stations for action!"

At the command we leaped to our posts—a futile gesture, considering what we had to fight with; but the training at the Academy made it instinctive for Bob and me, and old Gideon had spent too many years under the sea to fail to act without thinking at the word of command.

The little sea-car lurched and groaned as my uncle gave hard emergency right rudder and at the same time backed the inboard screws. We were turning to fight! If it was ramming they wanted, we could give it to them—not the gentle nudge from behind that would collapse our tired plates and let them go free, but a jolting, grinding head-on collision that would stove both our sea-cars in like eggshells and let the Deeps take us all at once!

The pursuer veered off like a skittish trout when the dry-fly takes an unexpected jump. They swung away, outside our curve of turn, and matched our emergency rudder in the other direction. On a battle chart the courses of the two sea-cars would have looked like two lobes of a fleur-de-lis, each of us swinging away and completely around, two hundred and seventy degrees; and at the end of the turn, we were headed directly for each other, scant scores of yards apart, arrowing in to certain destruction for us both.

They gave way. Stewart had known it would happen; he had been alert for the faint twitch in the microsonar trace that would indicate the split second when Hallam Sperry's hand faltered on the controls and tried to avert the crash that would destroy both craft. He saw it, and he spun the wheel to match it, desperately determined to meet them bow-to-bow. But our engines were weary, and theirs were powered for endless leagues of submarine cruising. Strain as we might, we couldn't quite catch them before they made their turn.

And then we were streaming straight-line through the vast deeps again, pursuer and pursued. But the tables were turned, for we were pursuing and they were running with all the force of their engines!

Stewart Eden grinned his fighting grin. In his hoarse, chuckling whisper he said, "It's worth it, boy, it's worth ending this way, just to see Hallam Sperry turn tail and run. Ah, bless the man, I could almost forgive him for the sake of this moment!"

"But we can't ram him this way!" I objected. "The speed differential isn't enough—we'd start our own plates, and hardly touch him!"

"As to that," chuckled Stewart Eden, "I have a trick or two. Watch his trace, boy! He's running crazy—not straight and true, but veering a little. If he loses two knots on us, if he just makes one run a fraction too far off course—trust me! I'll nail him!"

It was true. The course of the Sperrys' ship was nothing like arrow-true. There were hesitant dartings to one side and the other, up and down—not evasive tactics, not as we learned them in the Academy, but what seemed to be plain indecision, as though whoever was at the controls was faltering under the strain, unable to make the right move, afraid to make the wrong.

It was hard to understand. . . .

And the moment came. The fleeing sea-car swerved two points to starboard, hesitated, came back, swerved again. Not much loss in speed, but enough! For my uncle had designed enough sea-cars to know tricks that were not in the manuals; he brought one hand crashing down on the emergency-disconnect panel, and instantly we were plunged in darkness. Every light in the sea-car went dead, every inboard engine stopped. The ballast pumps halted; the air circulator fans rolled still, the heating coils faded, even the instrument lights went out. There wasn't a light or a sound inside our little car.

And every watt of power that was saved went direct into the throbbing engines.

It gave us barely two more knots of speed; and Stewart, without the microsonar greenish glow, was navigating blind. But we lunged ahead.

And we connected.

There was a horrible rattling screech from ahead—our bow planes tangling with the screws of the enemy. Our sea-car shuddered and bucked, and then plunged free.

As soon as we had disengaged, Stewart slapped the inboard circuits back into life again and peered anxiously into the microsonar.

"Stirred them up that time!" he gloated. "Look at them roll!"

Roll they did. The fading green trace showed the Sperrys' craft spiralling crazily through the sea. We had shattered one of their screws, perhaps fouled their stern diving planes. The damage could not have been fatal; but it had them temporarily out of control.

But our own ship—the returning light showed trouble! Where before there had been tiny fountains, feathering into mist, now there was a roaring, pounding stream at the edge of one of the forward bulkheads. Gideon leaped to scan the damage.

"It's bad," he reported, his face grave. "If we could surface right now, we might limp home——"

Stewart Eden shook his head. "Sorry, Gideon," he whispered. "Look at the microsonar."

We all looked, and we all knew that this was the end. The crazy spiral of the Sperry sea-car had straightened out; they were on our course, a quarter of a mile below us and far to the west, but they were coming up and back at nearly full speed. Whatever damage we had done had hardly cut their maximum speed by a quarter.

And we—were filling. At surface, we could pump and float; but at any depth at all we were doomed, even if they didn't reach us to ram us again—and ram us they easily could. For with the added weight of water our craft was loggy and slow.

Ram us they easily could. But they didn't.

While we watched, the trace of the other sea-car came driving up to our level; it came up, rounding out and over like an ancient aircraft doing a loop-the-loop. And, like that same aircraft, it barreled up and over and down again. It streaked down the long watery inclines, driving full-speed for the Deeps. Down and down and down, until the microsonar lost it.

"What in the world——" gasped Bob Eskow. None of us had an answer.

"Maybe—maybe we damaged them more than we thought," I guessed. My uncle shook his head.

"No," he said, "but——"

But there was no way of accounting for what they were doing. We stared, and we didn't believe what we saw. . . .

I think that, perhaps, I know what happened inside that sea-car. I remember Brand Sperry, on that first day at the Academy. He was strict and severe, a cadet-martinet. But he was not a thief, not a criminal. And when he found out that his father was all of the things the Academy had taught him to hate, when he learned that his family's rule of Marinia depended on blood and terror and underhanded dealings, I think that perhaps something inside him finally said sternly: "No! No farther than this!" And I think that when the sea-car wavered as it fled us, it was not a struggle of the helmsman to make up his mind, but perhaps a struggle between father and son, silent and deadly there under the deep Pacific waters, for command. And when the sea-car regained control and came up and over and down . . . there, I think, is the moment when the son won——

And lost.

A flickering spot came weaving up into the microsonar screen. "It's them!" cried Bob Eskow. "They're coming back!"

But my uncle Stewart was wiser than he. He stared deep into the pale glowing screen and shook his head.

Unhurriedly he set the sea-car on a gentle upward course, easy and slow, saving driving power to give extra energy to the hard-fighting pumps.

"The sea-car?" he asked. "No. Not exactly, Bob. Take a good look at the screen."

We looked, all of us.

It was no sea-car, that wavering, shapeless mass. It looked like—it was—a bubble of air, shuddering and wobbling, driving mindlessly to the surface.

A bubble of air. Stove plates, and a wrecked ship, and nothing to come to the surface to mark the death of a father and son but a bubble of air. . . .

We surfaced and set course for Fisherman's Island, where we could be picked up for the return trip to Thetis.

21

The Long Voyage

Fisherman's Island hadn't changed. We moored at almost the same spot on the coral reef as before, and Bob got busy on the communicator while we set the pumps to draining the last drops of seepage.

Bob looked worriedly up at me. "The only acknowledgment I get from Thetis," he said, "is 'Stand by for boarding.' It doesn't sound right, Jim."

My uncle Stewart rubbed his long jaw. "It isn't right," he said softly. "We've chopped off the head of the octopus, boys, but the arms are something else again. The Sperrys are out of the way, but the men they put in power are still in Thetis."

"You mean you think Sperry's sea-police will make trouble for us?" I asked.

"Think it, boy?" My uncle waved at the microsonar screen. "What do you make of that?"

There was something there, all right, big and distant but coming up fast. "I can't make it out," I said. "It—it doesn't look like a Marinian police vessel, and it's too fast for a tramp freighter."

Stewart Eden peered into the viewplate and shook his head. "I don't know, boy," he said in his soft voice. "No, it's not Marinian—not unless they've laid some new keels while I was tucked away at the bottom of the Deep. Whatever it is, we'll know soon enough."

The ship was literally boiling through the water toward us; perhaps *Isle of Spain* or another crack passenger liner might have made as many knots, but we were far from the liner routes.

Gideon coughed and said, "What happens if it *is* the sea-police?"

"Trouble, maybe," my uncle said grimly. "It depends." He looked at me with sober humor. "You didn't bargain on this, did you, Jim? I didn't mean to get you into it. I had other plans for you—plenty of money, out of the royalties on the new Edenite, the mines at the bottom of the Deep. But we can't always know how things will work out."

"But you still have all that, Mr. Eden!" Bob said.

Stewart Eden shook his head, the wry smile still on his lips. "Our lease on the Deep expires—Hallam Sperry's little trick of putting me out of the way for a while took care of that. And the new Edenite—I gave that away. I can't take it back." He patted me on the shoulder and winked. "Wouldn't if I could," he said. "There's money to be made and things to do. If we need the money, we'll earn it. If we don't—why, what is the use of having it?"

I said very sincerely, "Uncle Stewart, I never wanted the money, and I don't want it now. What I wanted most of anything in the world I got."

Stewart Eden looked at me for a moment, and then he looked away. We Edens don't show our feelings much; he didn't say anything; and he didn't have to.

Gideon said, "Whatever it is that's coming, it's within the thousand-yard range now!"

We swung to look at the microsonar, Gideon and Bob and I with apprehension, my uncle Stewart with a half smile. I couldn't understand it for a moment—it was not like my uncle to sit quiet and careless when an unknown danger was coming close. I stared, perplexed. . . .

Bob Eskow said tensely, "Think it's the sea-police?"

To my astonishment, my uncle was grinning broadly

now. He must have seen the perplexity in my eyes, because he laughed and said, "No, Bob, it isn't the sea-police. What in the seven seas did they teach you at that Academy, anyhow?"

Bob and I looked at each other for a moment, then, with the same impulse stared again at the screen—unbelieving, then sure.

"Of course!" said Bob, and even Gideon leaned back and sighed a long, relaxed sigh.

We scrambled out of the hatchway and up on deck in time to greet the upthrust nose of the long, gray silhouette of the *Nares*, flagship of the Marinian Patrol Command of the Sub-Sea Fleet.

The *Nares* was commanded by Fleet Captain Bogardus, a stern-faced four-striper with a chest full of ribbons and eyes of piercing black. We were escorted to the command cabin with full military honors, including a guard of armed seamen in full dress.

They didn't say whether they were a guard of honor or a prisoner-detail, and I, for one, didn't quite want to ask.

Bob and I saluted the captain with all of the snap and precision the Academy had given us. Gideon and my uncle were less formal. My uncle said, "Thanks for picking us up, Captain. You've done us a favor."

"That," the captain said frostily, "remains to be seen. It may interest you to know that the governor of Marinia has ordered this command to pick you up."

"I appreciate his concern," my uncle said gravely.

"Indeed." The captain nodded with a brisk motion. "You may sit down, gentlemen. I need hardly say that you've stirred up quite a commotion over the past few hours. Accusations against the mayor of Thetis——"

"The *late* mayor of Thetis," my uncle interrupted politely.

"The *late* mayor, then. All right. But he was a responsible public official, all the same, and if he is dead the circumstances concerning that death must be gone into very deeply, Mr. Eden. As, of course, must your allegation that he and his son were endeavoring to ram and destroy you."

"Of course," my uncle said shortly. He might have gone on from there, but Fleet Captain Bogardus held up his hand, and for the first time his expression seemed a trifle less frosty.

"On the other hand," he went on, "I need hardly say, Mr. Eden, that your word has a certain amount of weight too. Now, suppose you begin at the beginning and tell me just what all this hullabaloo is about. . . ."

We were in his office for an hour or more, while the captain asked questions and listened, and a methodical seaman took all our conversation down on a dictating machine. Then the Fleet Captain, courteously but blank-faced, excused himself and left us alone for a little while longer.

It wasn't for long. Bob had hardly had time to get restless when we heard the sharp crack of heels in the corridor outside and Fleet Captain Bogardus came in through the door.

"I've been in touch with the governor of Marinia," he said crisply. "I have my orders, gentlemen. We are already on course to Thetis!"

A fast cruiser of the Sub-Sea Fleet eats up the miles like no other vessel under the surface of the sea. We had time to eat and get a little cleaned up, and we were there.

And my uncle and I set out to clean up unfinished business.

We went to a certain place and opened a certain door, and the man behind the door jumped up, staring at us as though we were ghosts.

"Stewart Eden!" he gasped.

"The same," said my uncle. "What's the matter, Faulkner? Did you think I was out of the way for good?"

The lawyer sat down suddenly, breathing heavily. "My—my heart," he gasped. "This shock——"

"Too bad," said my uncle sharply. "We've had a few shocks too. Do you recognize my nephew here, the man you tried to have killed?"

Faulkner was getting a grip on himself. "Have killed?" he repeated. "Nonsense. This young man came around and tried to cause trouble, but I certainly—— Besides, he's not your nephew. He's an imposter! I've seen the real James Eden, and——"

"That's enough, Faulkner!" Stewart Eden's quiet voice was a whiplash. He towered over the white-lipped man, looking like some avenging sea-god about to strike down an infidel. "We've had lies enough out of you, Faulkner," my uncle snapped. "Now we'll take the truth. All of it!"

The man licked his lips. "What—what do you want?" he asked.

"The truth," my uncle repeated, like the tolling of some sea-bell. "The truth, Faulkner, the truth! The truth about you and Hallam Sperry, for a start. You were my lawyer, Faulkner, taking my money. And all the while you were secretly hand-in-glove with Sperry, selling me out to him, working with him in every shady deal in Thetis. Is that the truth, Faulkner?"

The man said feebly, "I—I——"

"Is it the truth?"

Faulkner swallowed. "Yes."

"In fact," my uncle went on remorselessly, "you helped Sperry take power in Thetis, didn't you? You sold out my Edenite patents to him and framed the contract so I lost control and lost my royalties. True? And with the money and power that gave him, you helped him build an empire here under the sea."

Faulkner only nodded. He was staring at my uncle in fascination, like a bird at a cobra, helpless and unable to move.

"And then Sperry got me out of the way," said Stewart Eden, "and Jim here came along. You tried to scare him off with crazy lies about sea-monsters. When he wouldn't scare, you tried to buy him out. When he wouldn't sell, you tried to kill him. When you couldn't kill him, you hired some cheap cut-purse from Kelly's Kingdom to impersonate him. Am I right, Faulkner?"

There was something glittering in Faulkner's eyes now, something that hadn't been there before. He was still looking at my uncle, but from time to time his eyes skipped past my uncle, to the door—the door that was moving slightly as though there were someone waiting on the other side of it.

Faulkner said viciously, "Right, Eden? Of course you're right! You and your nephew are two fools from the same hatch—and neither one of you deserves power or money, it's wasted on you!" He stood up and leaned forward, over the desk, staring piercingly at my uncle. "Do you doubt it, Eden?" he demanded. "Let me show you! You came in here, but you may not find it so easy to get out alive. Take a look at that door, Eden! I've standing orders here: When there's unwelcome company in the office, my man Bishop waits there to show them out when the time comes. And that time is now! *Bishop, shoot them down!*"

He shouted the last words on a note of triumph. But the triumph didn't last. Quick as the lashing stroke of a hammerhead, my uncle leaped to the door and flung it wide. "Your man has other engagements, Faulkner," he cried. "See for yourself!"

And Faulkner, staring in a moment of horror and unbelief at his Neanderthal doorman, helpless in the grip of two sturdy men of the Sub-Sea Fleet while an armed squad of others stood at the ready before him, slumped slowly and finally to the desk. . . .

With Thetis under martial law—established by Fleet Captain Bogardus at the radioed order of the governor of Marinia—a new day opened up for all of us. The Sperrys were gone; Faulkner and his staff and a few score others were under lock and key; and the power of the Sperrys', like a sea-sorcerer's spell, vanished in a bubble of froth.

Even the Sub-Sea Fleet's martial law was hardly needed, after those first hours—it stayed on only long enough for new and free elections to be held.

It didn't take long. Only a few days after the Sub-Sea Fleet had ringed Thetis and cleaned out the last of the Sperry influence, Bob Eskow and I walked down one of the broad ways between long lines of citizens of Thetis, casting their ballots. There was no trouble. Every polling booth was guarded by a detachment from the Sub-Sea Fleet, the bright scarlet uniforms of the Western Allies, the sea-blue and fouled anchors of the European Union, even the sea-bottom gray of the Asian Command. Every component of the Sub-Sea Fleet was represented in the Marinian Patrol Command; and all of them took turn and turn about in policing Thetis.

Neither Bob nor I said a word; but I could tell what he was thinking as we looked at the smart submariners. The closest Bob came to saying what was in both our hearts was when he sighed and said, "With the Sperrys out of business, I guess I'm out of a job."

I nodded. "And I guess I'd better start looking for one."

And that seemed to be that. . . .

Until, returning to the hotel where we shared quarters with my uncle, we found a message waiting for us: "Report to Fleet Captain Bogardus without delay."

My uncle was in the Captain's command room, waiting for us and there was a smile on his face. Perhaps I should have guessed—but I didn't. It was only when the captain handed me the familiar platinum-crested envelope that I began to suspect. "The Sub-Sea Fleet doesn't often make a mistake," he said, "but when it does, it *always* admits it. When you two resigned, it was under pressure—and there's no doubt, now, that a lot of the pressure was more than improper. So—well, this is from the Academy, for both of you. Open it up."

The words danced in front of my eyes as I held the sheet of paper up before me. "In view of new information," it said, and, "resignation disapproved," and, most important of all, the last sentence, unbelievable but clear before my eyes:

"Cadets Eden, J., and Eskow, R., will therefore proceed by fastest available transportation to the Academy to resume training. By order of the Commandant, U.S.S.S."

We were reinstated!

Bob and I found ourselves in the passageway outside the command cabin, half dazed. We looked at each other incredulously.

"Well," I said, trying to seem unemotional about it, "it looks like we won't have to worry about a job for a while."

"Sure," he said, poker-faced as I. . . . And then his broad face split in a grin. "Who are you kidding?" he demanded exuberantly. "Jim, we made it, we made it! Let's get going, lubber—we've got packing to do. And *the tides won't wait!*"